I0456764

Stonewall Against Las Vegas

A Shattered Moon Novel

Joseph Browning

Text Copyright © 2019 by Joseph Browning

Published by Expeditious Retreat Press
Cover by Vivid Covers
Edited by Elizabeth VanZwolle

For information regarding Joseph Browning's novels and to subscribe to his mailing list, see his website at https://www.joseph-browning.com

To follow Joseph on Twitter: https://twitter.com/Joseph_Browning

To follow Joseph on Facebook: https://www.facebook.com/joseph.browning.52

To follow Joseph on MeWee: https://mewe.com/i/josephbrowning

By Joseph Browning

SHATTERED MOON NOVELS: STONEWALL SERIES
Stonewall Against the Rat Men
Stonewall Against the Vulture Men
Stonewall Against Las Vegas
Stonewall Against the Center Sea

Chapter One

Our Story So Far

Everything was fine until I won an all-expenses-paid vacation to Las Vegas. I know, I know, all expenses weren't paid, nor was it a vacation, but let's be honest; if you had a hologram from the ancients telling you that you and your family were heading to Vegas, and then it actually teleported you there, you'd say the same.

I'd like to tell you the teleportation was a pleasant affair—I'd also like a cold six-pack and a 16 oz Porterhouse while I'm at it—but after watching the ephemeral images of Vegas shimmering against the Waukegan skyline—sans the Lancaster Building—I transitioned from feeling fine to on my knees and puking in less than a minute. I blacked out and woke up on the top floor of a skeletonized casino overlooking the walls of the only city in what's now called the Lucky Duchy. Oh, and it was 104°F, because of course it was.

On the positive side, at least I wasn't alone; Zew and Diana were with me. Apparently, the silver globe that projected the hologram and teleported us here thought they were my family. When I say "positive," I'm speaking quite selfishly—I mean,

I'm *positively* sure that Zew and Diana would have rather I'd gone alone and left them safely behind in Deeplac.

Diana is a green-scaled near-human only an inch or two shorter than myself. She's known as the Blade Witch because she can't be injured by sharp objects, and worse, if you try, you'll end up hurting yourself instead. I've seen more than a few sentients accidentally and unintentionally commit suicide because of her ability.

Zew is a barbarian who'd walked out of the wasteland into our little society less than two years ago. He is six feet tall, his muscles have muscles, and he favors a florescent Mohawk. He too is scaly, but not as much as Diana, and his scales are—for lack of a better word—human-colored. He is preternaturally resistant to all damage; he can shake off things that would kill a normal creature.

Another bright spot was that we still had everything we'd been carrying. At least we weren't teleported naked. I had my trusty M1B plasma blaster with sixty-two shots left, as well as my M24 sniper rifle with scope and 105 rounds. I'd loaded out heavy before my explosives mission against the vulture men, and it paid off in an unexpected way. My typical gear was intact—my ratty body armor, adaptive ghillie suit, plasma cutter, KM6800 fighting utility knife, and my binoculars—capable of both low-light and infrared vision. Additionally, I still had possession of Marilyn's crafted silvery leather gloves. They created an anti-gravity field around heavy magnetic metal objects that allowed me to pick up 200 pounds as if it wasn't there, and also let me to hang onto magnetic metal with the slightest applied strength, meaning I could climb most metal structures without having to worry about keeping my grip. Money-wise, I had six gold eagles and a bag of trade goods. Actually, I had eight gold eagles—Deeplac wasn't going to get a share of the coins that we found just before our teleportation.

Zew and Diana still had their normal kit as well as the additional gold and trading goods. Zew favored his spear and Diana her two swords, although both had rifles with scopes as well as the repurposed-rebar knife everyone seems to have. I didn't know if they had any additional unique gear, and it wasn't my place to ask.

On the negative side, none of us had rope, except the spare twenty feet of thin high-tensile stuff Zew kept wrapped up around his waist as a sort of belt. We only had two days of food each and enough water in our canteens for a single day in this heat; we hadn't expected to be gone for more than a few hours.

And we still had the silver sphere, which was an enigma in-and-of-itself. It was about the size of a softball and no longer warmed to anyone's touch. I don't know why the sphere decided we were the winners of a contest that expired who knows how long ago, nor do I know how the sphere had managed to come into the possession of the vulture men we had just recently destroyed. For that matter, I don't know why the sphere hadn't activated until I touched it. But I do know that's life beneath the shattered moon; you accept that reality has a chip on its shoulder, a bad case of cataracts, and a monumental indifference to whatever plan you had.

Chapter Two

Eyeing Las Vegas

"What the...?"

"How'd we...?"

"It's not my fault."

"It's definitely your fault, Stonewall," Diana said adamantly, shaking her head clear from the teleportation. "We just don't know how yet."

"I believe that's Las Vegas," Zew said, standing up in the blaring heat and pointing to a walled settlement two miles north of us. He seemed insensate to the physical effects Diana and I were feeling. We turned to look. From our thirty-sixth-story view, we saw a thick wall made of adobe, encased in thousands of automobile hoods, tops, and trunk doors that excised a space within the ruins of what was once the decadence capital of the world. The wall sprawled and curved, encircling several miles of desert land within which rested the largest post-apocalypse settlement I'd ever seen. There was enough space for tens of thousands of sentients, if you could feed and water them.

I compared my view with the maps of Las Vegas I had in my memory storage and located where I was. "It's Vegas, all right. That skeletal pyramid was the Luxor Hotel."

"What's that?" Diana asked, indicating a small, recently installed brass plaque bolted onto a concrete pillar. The plaque bore an inscription:

Forgive my intrusion upon your mighty work and I welcome you to Las Vegas, Great and Powerful Wizard! We seek an audience with you. Please bring your silver globe to the gates of Las Vegas and we will escort you to my palace for a truly great offer that you simply can't refuse.

His Magnificent Gamblence, Royal Flush

"Still think it's my fault?"

"Shut up, Stonewall."

"I don't think we should follow the plaque's advice," Zew voiced caution.

"Yeah, I don't think it's our best option right now," I agreed. "That may change in the future, though."

Diana looked at the silver globe she still held. "Didn't the recording say two weeks?"

I nodded.

"Shouldn't we just wait until then and see what happens? Maybe it will transport us back."

"It's worth a shot." Zew shrugged.

"We don't have enough food or water to last that long out

here." I shaded my eyes, "Speaking of which, how about we go down a level and get out of the sun so we can think about this?"

We found the stairwell. "They repaired this section," I said, pointing out a recent fix on the descent, "so it should be an easy way to the ground." Passing through a door labeled "35," we debouched one level below and enjoyed the shade provided by the dusty concrete above us.

I had been to Vegas in my time, but that wasn't going to help much in the present, and I didn't know much about the extended history of either Diana or Zew. Looking over the distant city, I asked, "Have either of you been here before?"

Diana shook her head but Zew answered, "I have, but it was a long time ago. From the look of things, a lot has changed since then."

Our elevation made a perfect vantage point, and I passed around my binoculars so everyone could get a better view of the place. There were three large gatehouses on the east, south, and north sides through which traffic huddled. The southern and eastern gatehouses were the busiest. Large crowds were bunched up around them, like water before a narrow channel. Paths led from the gates and travelers passed in both directions, forming a nearly unbroken line a mile long before distance and time finally spread them apart from each other. Without my binoculars, the black robes favored by the travelers resembled ants walking along their scent trail. There were thousands of sentients down there in gate traffic alone.

Unlike the other gates, the north gatehouse was closed and two paths diverged beyond it, one heading north and the other east. Both trails bore the unmistakable double-rut created by wheeled internal combustions vehicles. While most of the roads were hidden by layers of dirt, the roadways out of the northern gate were worn down to the pavement; there was a lot of vehicular traffic passing through that exit.

"That's just amazing," Diana remarked after we'd taken it all in. "There are more sentients down there then I've seen in my life."

Zew nodded. "Las Vegas is the only safe place between the Colorado Kingdoms, the Crusader States of California, and the Texan Hegemony. Every major trading company has a permanent house there, as do all the major secret societies."

I did an about face, surprised by his knowledge.

He looked at me. "I've been around."

"Secret societies?"

"The Church of Parkour is probably the only one you've heard of. They're trustworthy."

"What are the others?" I pressed.

He paused and gathered his thoughts. "The Firemen, the Combine of Exquisite Smiles, the Back and the Thigh, the Holy Coterie of Delmar Louis, the Laughter at the End of Time, and the Order of Cybernetic Magnificence are probably all down there in some form. As well as the ZZZ Society and the Brotherhood of Pure Thought—they're the other two worth trusting, but only if you're bargaining from a position of power."

As Zew listed off the societies, Diana nodded her head to a few of them, indicating she'd heard of them as well.

"Not very secret if everyone knows about them," I quipped.

"Just because you know their name doesn't mean you know anything about them. The Church of Parkour is the most open of them, and they're still secretive as hell. You've got to be a member of their society to know what's really going on."

A trail of dust rose in the east as he finished and I turned the binoculars on it. Three tanker trucks escorted by a cadre of punked-out automobiles drove toward the north gate. I pointed them out to Diana and Zew, "My bet is water or gasoline. Each one could hold 8,000 gallons of either."

It had been a long time since I saw a group of functioning vehicles and my training kicked in. I identified the make and model of each vehicle that passed, running through their capabilities and limitations just like I used to do when I was an assassin for The Company. I shook my head once I realized what I was doing. Even though the information could be useful, I wasn't an aimed weapon anymore; I'm a free agent, not on a mission.

I take that back, I am on a mission: to return to Deeplac. I've 1,800 miles to go, but I'll get there.

I handed the binoculars over to Diana so she could watch the convoys. They were new to her and exciting. "I've seen a few before, but nothing like those big ones," she referred to the tractor-trailers. "I've seen shells of them, of course, but *moving...*"

"There were millions of them before the moon split," I mused. "Many of them even drove themselves, transporting goods from place to place like bees flying in and out of a hive."

She looked at my face to see if I was kidding her, but quickly turned back to the entrancing combustion vehicles.

Zew, on the other hand, wasn't particularly interested in cars. He was looking at the southern gate. "What's that big wheel in front of that gate?"

Diana turned the binoculars toward the gate. "It's a spinner of some sort." She watched a bit more and added, "Looks like some people lined up to enter the city are spinning it."

Great—a game of chance, perhaps, with the ones of the prizes entering Vegas? What could go wrong? I thought to myself.

"Can I look?" Zew inquired.

Diana handed the binoculars over to him for a look. "Yeah, I can't see what's on it, but it looks like writing of some sort. Wait...the wheel just stopped and they're dragging someone off through the gates."

"We won't be able to tell what it is until we're closer," I surmised. "Speaking of which, we've got about four hours till sundown and I think I'd rather err on the side of caution and spend the night on the inside of the wall rather than outside, unless either of you feel differently?"

"I don't," Diana stated.

"I'd prefer being inside as well," Zew said. "We should get going soon; it'll take an hour to get there and I don't know how long it will take to get through the gate."

"Let's wait a little longer to see what we are getting into," I suggested and they agreed. We handed the binoculars back and forth for the next half hour, watching the sentients enter and leave the city. Two more convoys of tanker trucks returned via the north gate as we spied; if the Hoover Dam was standing, even partially, there'd still be Lake Mead east of Las Vegas for fresh water.

From our position, we could see several different sections of the city, along with areas of interior fortification. Near the eastern and southern gates, construction was ramshackle and small, filled with thousands of small buildings made from recycled scrap. A single main street went from each of the gatehouses to a large center square filled with stalls and large buildings, presumably warehouses for the goods flowing through Las Vegas.

Away from the gates and main streets, large fortified structures littered the city; houses of the individually wealthy or strongholds of trading companies or secret societies. The traffic was less congested outside the main thoroughfares but constant nonetheless, sometimes vehicular in nature although bicycles and other sentient-powered transports were more common. A few of the large buildings had a constant flux of movement both in and out, so I marked those down as governmental or possibly religious structures.

Of particular note was a large colosseum built of adobe and scrap. It could house at least fifty thousand and its sandy floor filled me with a sudden sense of dread. The interior wall was thirty feet off the ground, twice as high as the Flavian Amphitheater of Rome, and had several massive portcullises connected with interior chambers. There was only one reason why the gates would be that big: wild beast fights. Under the shattered moon, that could be just about anything.

Chapter Three

Intake and Upkeep

Eventually we decided we'd seen enough and started the walk down from the thirty-fifth floor. The stairwell was on the northern end of the building and open to the air, providing us a continual view of the city. As we descended, we were better able to judge the height of the various buildings within Las Vegas and gained a real appreciation of the sheer size of the colosseum.

"Was there a colosseum when you were here?" I asked Zew.

"It was being constructed. There were still matches, of course, but they didn't decide to build a giant fighting arena until after the competitions began."

"Who competes?"

"Most of the fighters are criminals," he said, carefully avoiding one of the many small holes in the staircase. "It usually took some sort of violent act to get thrown into the pit, but justice had few benchmarks or recourse when I was there; you could be sent to the fights for something as simple as theft if the sentient you'd stolen from was politically connected."

"How long were you there?" Diana angled for more

information.

"Several years," he answered tersely. He ran his hand across his forehead and over his mohawk; it was the first time I had seen him sweat since we arrived. "Look, if you're going to keep pressing me, I'd rather not play twenty questions." He stopped and looked directly at us, the angled sunlight casting deep shadows along his face. "I'm a lot older than I look. I was here about fifty years ago. As I said, a lot has changed. My information is very out of date and shouldn't be trusted."

If I had to guess Zew's age from his appearance, I would have gone with late-thirties, perhaps even younger since sentients here seem to age faster than they did in my time.

"And before you ask, I'm over one hundred years old. I'm not sure exactly, because a few years are bound to slip by without notice when you live long enough."

"All right," Diana said, her tone indicating that she wouldn't intrude anymore.

"Agreed, sorry to pry. If you think anything's important, just let us know," I added. Obviously, I wanted nothing more than to pry, but he'd likely be more willing to talk sometime when he wasn't so annoyed with us.

We made our way down the stairs in silence. The breeze at the top slowly died and the air warmed with each downward step until we stood upon the parched ground; the air was completely still and intensely hot. We headed north, passing through ruins that were so well picked-through, they were almost clean, which was unsurprising considering the number of sentients in the area. We attracted the attention of a small group that failed miserably to shadow us as we traveled toward the southern gate. The word "Exile" was prominently tattooed on their foreheads. If they were looking for easy prey, our rifles kept them at bay.

As we neared the city, we followed suit (from our observations) and turned west to join the end of the line—no one likes a cutter. We walked against the flow of inbound traffic; sentients of every sort stared at us, but even more ignored us. It had been so long since I was in a crowd larger than a few hundred people that I'd forgotten the feeling—that unique mix of acute observation coupled with utter indifference.

It was safe to say we stood out from the crowd, most notably our lack of suitable clothing. Nothing says "we're not from around here" than when you aren't dressed like the locals. Our clothing was far from garish, but everyone else was monochromatic: two-thirds wore black robes that blocked out the sun, much like the Bedouin did, while the remainder were in white, much like the Saudis. A few colorful splotches emerged, typically among reptilian sentients of which there were many; those with Gila monster backgrounds sparkled brightest in the radiant heat.

We queued up behind a group of eight traders of horned lizard ancestry. They eyed us but said nothing. They were armed with a mix of melee and missile weapons, bookending a cart pulled by a camel. It was generous to call it a cart; really, it was the back of an old pickup truck scavenged into a cart.

We'd only been in the line for a few minutes when another group got behind us. Composed of at least two dozen sentients, they were dressed in black and covered with dust. Hauling three Conestoga wagons packed to the gills with jagged pieces of metal poking out from all directions, I assumed they were scrappers pulling up whatever they could find for trade.

"Where'd you come from, friend?" one of the newcomers asked Diana in Spanish, a language that many standing in line were using. He was a near-human, scaled much like she was, but he was a dark gray-green color, nearly slate.

She glared at him with a blank face, so he repeated his question in English.

"Oshkosh," she generalized, uninterested in where this conversation was going.

"Oskhosh...er, Oshkosh," he said, eying more than her bag of trade goods. "Can't say I've heard of Oshkosh before."

"It's west of Lake Michigan."

"Lake Michigan! You're a long way from home. Need someone to show you around? I know all the good spots—"

"Already got a guide." Diana nodded her head at Zew. "He's showing us around."

"You local, friend?" he asked Zew.

Zew's piercing eyes bored into him as he responded, "Might as well be."

If scaled-guy was confused by that answer, it didn't show. "I can hook you up with the best guide in Las Vegas." He smiled and pointed to himself with his thumbs. "Emilio Martinez. I can get you a good daily rate, twenty percent off the normal charge." Although he was ostensibly responding to Zew, he was looking at Diana.

"No thanks, Emilio. As I said before, already got a guide," she firmly rebuffed his offer.

"Well, if you change your mind before you pass the gate, let me know," the scaled-guy pressed before quickly turning around to check on his wagons.

Diana chuckled and Zew cracked a smile. I'd suspected as much, but that was a pretty good confirmation.

The line progressed at a decent clip. The closer we got to the gate, the noise of the crowd became a constant soft roar punctuated by blasts of applause and less frequent groans. Once we rounded the last tower, we found the source of the clamor: the wheel.

The wheel was mounted on an elevated platform parallel to the gates. A painted sign hung above it, declaring in English and Spanish: "If you're short of a buck, spin the wheel and try your luck!" A ring of pins on the outer circumferential edge demarcated the thirty wedges of fate that ticked against the pointer: fight (2), exile (2), a year's labor (2), a month's labor (2), a week's labor (2), water guard (2), a day's labor (4), lose an item (4), spin again (1), welcome! (7), gain a silver lady

(1), gain a gold eagle (1). None of the similar sections abutted each other and each positive outcome was separated by at least one negative outcome. A cadre of guards manned the gate and the platform. They were all dressed in black robes with an embroidered playing card on the breast and a differing series of colored bands on the arms.

It didn't take long before someone tested their luck, and he was led onto the platform for a spin. The crowd hushed as the heavy disk spun, and the clicking of metal pins against the needle progressively slowed until it landed on "Fight." The crowd went wild with applause, laughing and cheering the bad lack of the poor sap, who was dragged away by three of the guards.

"That's new," Zew noted drily, as if the novelty of the wheel was the most noteworthy thing about the whole affair.

The crowd thickened as we neared the gates. The queues lost their cohesion and broke into a mob that, while not physically pushy, required individual initiative to reach the front.

"How many in your group?" a bored guard asked when we finally arrived.

"Three," Zew responded. We'd agreed he'd speak for us.

"Pay your lady and surrender your weapons."

Zew went first, plopping a silver lady on the counter followed by his assortment of weapons. Each weapon was tagged with a label and given a number before they were confiscated. In exchange, we were given tickets that matched the tagged labels. Diana and I followed his lead as we were escorted through the main gates and down a long corridor to another guard.

The passageway opened into a room filled with chairs in which entrants sat, each getting an automated tattoo from a long arm-like structured tipped with a tattoo gun. The corresponding number of their weapons were being inked onto their owners.

"An effective way to reduce fraud," I remarked.

The guard ignored my comment while he checked each of us in by name and a list of associated item numbers. After a moment, he took our tickets and handed each of us a bar code.

"Go sit down on a chair and put the lines in front of the red light," he instructed.

I found a chair and scanned the code while Zew and Diana walked further down the line to grab two chairs that were next to each other. The automated tattoo apparatus whipped around and two clamps held my left arm down while it applied a list of numbers associated with my various weapons. It was painful, but no worse than a regular tattoo.

As the machine tattooed my last number, red lights started flashing from both Zew's and Diana's chairs. Two guards rushed to each of them, cursing. "Why didn't you tell us you were resisters?"

Zew calmly responded, "We weren't asked."

"Now we gotta get new needles, you idiots! You owe us a

lady each for the replacements."

Again, Zew replied as if someone had inquired about the weather, "Certainly. We'll need to make change."

The guard fumed but made change as required. Diana and Zew were each fitted with a snug steel necklace from which a small locked metal box hung. Within the box, the guard placed a series of small numbered metal plates, each number corresponding to one of their checked weapons.

Once we were finished, they kicked us out onto the main thoroughfare of Las Vegas, the part of old South Las Vegas Boulevard where it crossed Tropicana, and told us to go to pedestrian customs to declare our other valuable items.

The first thing that hit me was the smell—the unique mélange of sweaty bodies, food, perfumes, and excrement that came with densely populated areas. The narrow but deep channels of gravity-driven excrement lined the streets, thankfully covered, but their presence was betrayed by the scent. After recovering from the initial assault of odors, I noticed that everyone but us was armed. Clearly, we were missing something important.

A large section of the main road near the gate was partitioned for customs and we headed in that direction before we realized it was transport vehicles only and were directed to the other side of the street. A brief peek past the guard revealed a remarkable variety of non-motorized conveyances, with camels and a strange sort of lizard-turtle hybrid being the most common. It appeared all the motorized vehicles used the north gate, where there was presumably a refueling station.

The press in and out of pedestrian customs was nearly as intense as it had been at the gate, but we made our way though and declared everything of value in our possession. They were particularly interested in my plasma cutter. As I did at weapons check, I only demonstrated it as a joined cutter and omitted the straight cutter option. As a joined cutter, it was obviously a tool and not a weapon, since the cutting edge was only an inch long; however the straight cutter could produce a four-inch field of plasma that could easily be used as a weapon. I saw no reason to be completely honest.

My concern about the silver sphere in Diana's possession did not come to fruition; apparently the customs guards didn't get the same memo as the gate guards. Diana had very carefully avoided showing the sphere to the gate guards, not wanting a so-called escort to the palace. It didn't hurt that Diana described it as "junk" when asked, and stated her intent to scrap it right away. They passed it by without a second thought and continued with the remaining contents in her bag.

We were assessed a tax roughly amounting to another silver lady. I guess now's as good a time as any to explain how money worked beneath the shattered moon. It came in two widely accepted forms, both based off the 1 oz bullion coins struck by the US mint. Eagles referred to the gold 1 oz coin and ladies the silver 1 oz coin. The number of ladies to an eagle varied, but it's usually in the fourteen to seventeen range. Making change was done the old-fashioned way: venders kept sturdy shears on hand and the coins were deftly cut into slices like a pizza—up to eighths—and then weighed to ensure the transaction was good. Therefore, a pocket full of change was composed of various slices of different coins.

I had seen the gold coins of other nations, like the South African Krugerrand, Canadian Maple, and Chinese Panda freely exchanged with the eagle. I imagined that platinum coins sometimes circulated, as must the copper coins the mint used to make, but I hadn't seen them. Ammunition was also used as currency, but we were holding onto ours and would only use it if we were out of eagles and ladies. I'm sure there were other forms of specie, but those were the most common.

After paying our taxes, we were given a stamped form and instructed to keep it on our person at all times, as it would be needed when we left. As I folded the paper and placed it within my interior belt pocket, it occurred to me that there must be a lucrative smuggling business in Las Vegas, both in materials and sentients. The punishment would no doubt be steep, but I got the impression that those who were politically connected would be insulated from consequences and therefore left to conduct the bulk of business. I might be out of my time, but some things never change.

Once we left the taxation area, we were assaulted by a mob of touts offering various services, one of the ubiquitous forms of graft in any city. After a brief consultation amongst ourselves, we decided on a near-human child no more than ten years old who offered guide service for a quarter lady a day, provided we were satisfied with her selections of a good cheap restaurant and a similar hotel. Her name was Soledad Martinez, and she instantly took our offer of a four-day orientation and overview of the city.

"But first, you want to rent some weapons, right?" she proposed.

"Rent some weapons?" Diana asked.

"You know, to protect yourselves." She whipped out a small beaten rebar knife with a hempen handle and twirled it back and forth before us, as if we didn't understand what weapons were.

"Right," I confirmed. "Who's your recommendation for a weapons' lender?"

The girl laughed. "Only the duke rents weapons! I'll lead you there." She took off rapidly, weaving in and out of the crowd and finding holes where there were none. We had to hustle to follow, and I was certain that none of us could have caught her if she didn't want to be caught.

Our destination was three blocks away, although we'd passed several weapons' lenders along the way. Only melee weapons were available, so our selection was rather limited. When I commented on that, the vendor retorted that it was the duke's rule; only the duke's guards were allowed firearms or ranged weapons in the city. We each rented a spear and a rebar long knife for a lady each, half of which we'd get back when we returned them.

Standing at the counter, I asked Soledad, "Why didn't you stop at one of other lenders we passed along the way?"

"The lines are shorter here," she posited.

I stared at her. "And…?"

"And my Uncle Ignacio franchises this place, but you wouldn't have gotten better prices closer to the gate," she protested.

"He's not still in nappies," Ignacio said to Soledad in Spanish.

I smiled and responded to him in the same language, "No, I'm not."

He slapped his thigh and let out a barking laugh as his niece's face flushed. "I should have tried to charge you more!" His broad face widened. "We could have had a good bargaining session!"

Next, Soledad took us to a restaurant serving soup, tacos, and fried snacks. Zew and Diana dove into the food without thought, but I limited myself to the soup, hoping to ease my way into the new micro-faunal and micro-floral environment. The food was cheap and good, and given the resemblance between the cook and Soledad, I expected another uncle or cousin was at the helm.

Such proved to be the case. The restaurant and the hotel

next door—Hotel White House—were both owned by Soledad's parents. They greeted her with hugs and kisses as she brought us through the door, and they quickly processed us into two rooms with instructions on available services, such as laundry, small item acquisition, and clean prostitutes of any persuasion. They also proudly proclaimed that their water tank was checked weekly by a Geiger counter, which made me a little bit paranoid about everything else. We could even rent electricity via a plug behind the counter. A single bulb lit the central room, but the rest of the place wasn't wired. Kerosene lamps were used in the bedrooms.

"So, am I hired as a guide for the next four days?" Soledad asked Zew once all the arrangements were settled.

"You got the gig, kid," Zew said curtly, closing the door to his and Diana's room. "Wake us in the morning."

Chapter Four

The Belly of the Beast

Soledad was true to her word and woke us just as the sun was getting comfortable in the sky. We all went down for a delicious breakfast of beans and squash, served with a hearty helping of thick corn bread. As we ate, we arranged a weekly rate with both the cook and Soledad's parents for food and lodging.

We paid half up front and then followed our guide out into the cool rustling streets for what she thought would be the grand Las Vegas tour, but we had other plans. We requested she take us to the junker side of town, as we had trade goods that needed converting into coin. She did a decent job of masking her disappointment and perked up when Diana reassured her we'd take the grand tour afterward.

The junker side of town was north of the central market square, and we passed hundreds of non-motorized vehicles full of scrap as well as several major buildings along the way. Most prominent was the duke's castle near the center of town, whose walls were twins of the town walls: adobe covered with hammered car top and hoods. The walls soared forty feet in the air and were at least thirty feet thick, easily capable of resisting most cannon fire. The gatehouse was constructed from scavenged metal and gaped opened to allow easy movement of in-and-outbound traffic.

The other major structure on our stroll to the traders was the remains of the Eiffel Tower Experience. Only the first level had endured, bearing damage from where the upper levels once collapsed westward into the street. Smoke rose from within, somewhere in the middle of the closed platform.

"What's up there?" I asked, pointing to the curls of soot emanating from the tower.

"That's the crematory, where you go when you die." Soledad raised her tanned arm skyward. "They have big mirrors up there that burn you to ash, sending your smoke up to the sky." She traced a path downward, pointing to a large, lizard-pulled wagon located at the bottom of a chute beneath the center of the platform. "They take your ashes and ship them east to the Colorado States. They put them on the corn they grow there and sell it back to us." She tilted her head to let us in on a secret. "That cornbread you had this morning had someone's grandpa in it…" She was unperturbed by the whole affair, and her hushed tone at the end seemed more in reverence to the deceased than in shame or revulsion.

"He was a tasty old cuss," I joked and she smiled. Human ashes aren't that good for plants—too high in salt and calcium among other things—so I wondered what they were doing to the ashes to make them good for plants, or if they were using them for agriculture at all. At least the crematory took care of a disease vector.

Given yesterday's experience, I expected her to take us to another establishment owned by a relative, but it didn't look like the Martinez clan was in the scavenging business. Instead, she took us to the place her mother went whenever someone couldn't pay a bill and they had to confiscate their belongings. The proprietor, Crikloto, was of Gila monster stock, had four arms, and spoke slowly with a slight lisp.

We took turns unloading our bags of loot collected from the collapsed Lancaster Building onto a large metal table in the center of the intake area. Diana kept the silver sphere, but everything else she'd found went on the table. Crikloto walked around our pile, picking up some items for closer examination while ignoring others.

"I'll give you three eagles for the lot," he said after five minutes.

"Four," Zew said.

"Three eagles and nine ladies," Crikloto countered.

"Three eagles, nine ladies, and a lady for the kid." Zew nodded to Soledad, who was browsing bits of tat that struck her fancy.

Crikloto held out one of his hands and Zew shook, sealing the deal. I couldn't tell if he was being kind or simply priming our guide for future payoff—Zew's a hard one to read at the best of times. Not that it mattered to the youngest entrepreneur in the Martinez clan; she was as happy as a clam at high tide, and tucked her lady into a slit she'd cut in the interior of her wide leather belt. Smart kid.

With our bags lightened and our purses a little fuller, we gave Soledad free rein over where we went next, and she made a beeline through the narrow streets to the northwest part of the city to land on the stoop of an honest-to-God old-timey candy shop, complete with red-and-whited striped awning. As she pulled the door open, I could smell the sugar in the air, and the ringing bell drew the shopkeeper's attention. It wasn't a large space, and each vibrant confection sat in its own large glass container topped with a brass lid; the packed shelves painted the small room in a kaleidoscope of colors. Obviously the young Miss Martinez had her own ideas on how to spend her silver lady, but none of us argued with her. Sugar was very rare in Deeplac, and we all welcomed the opportunity for a bit of indulgence. It was an expensive luxury, but a pound of mixed hard candy in more than a dozen flavors made stepping back into the harsh sunlight that much more bearable.

Once everyone's sweet tooth was appeased, I suddenly realized what might be possible. "Soledad, you have to find us a coffee shop!" I loudly proclaimed my heart's desire to the surprised street. I'd had exactly one cup of coffee in nigh on two years, and it was the thing I missed most about my old world. My three companions looked at me like I was crazy, asking for a steaming cup of Joe in this heat.

Zew and Diana laughed at how genuinely excited I was at the prospect of real coffee and assured our guide I was normal-crazy, not sunstroke crazy. Soledad nodded, and off she went with me hot on her heels. She found a place a few blocks west of the main street, and I paid half a lady for an actual burr-ground Americano. It was heaven in a cup and I was willing to share, but when I offered a cup to Diana and Zew, they declined for a cold drink and candy. Apparently, they didn't share my appreciation of the dark bitter brew.

Next, Soledad led us to the colosseum for the first matches of the day. Every day, there were at least three matches before noon, and on special occasions there were night matches, mostly hosted by the big trading houses looking for the best fighters to staff their long-distance trade caravans. The first match of the day was always free, so Zew and Diana were willing to watch at least one match, but I wasn't interested in blood sports.

We parted ways outside one of the many giant entrances into the arena, with promises to meet back at the hotel restaurant for lunch in three hours. For the first time in a long time, I was alone in a strange city, surrounded by strange people. I went back to the coffee shop to savor another ridiculously expensive drink and think about what I wanted to do with the rest of my morning.

Between the maps from my past and the landmarks we had seen yesterday and this morning, I had a basic framework of a current Las Vegas map based upon the paths taken by Soledad. I'd mapped the street dimensions and orientation along with every single permanent and temporary vendor along the way. I couldn't help it—the computer in my head gave me exceptional abilities and I was going to make the most of them. Even though I had major thoroughfares outlined, I had big gaps of the areas in between, and felt the need to fill them in. Bolstered with caffeine and with no real purpose, I decided to walk about the city to flesh out the map in my head as the sun rose higher in the sky.

When confronted by a new location, most people get their bearings in a spider-web pattern, essentially creating an internal map by sticking close to what's familiar and then perambulating around that. If you were like most people, it made since—get your bearings with a minimal chance of getting lost. Thankfully, I didn't have that problem and could tactically explore a new location based upon an importance hierarchy.

In my mind, the most important part of Las Vegas wasn't the sentients, shops, food, the many religious spaces, the duke, or even the great trading houses. None of those were the lifeblood of the city—the vital substance which, if taken away, destroys the thing itself. No, that designation fell upon water and the fuel that allowed its transport into the city.

So my first destination was the north gate, as that was the entrance through which fuel and water flowed into Vegas. The entire north gate area was walled off via an internal wall twice my height, strictly off-limits to anyone not associated with the duke or one of the trading houses. Despite this setback, I could still look through the gates leading into the area and hunkered down against a wall to watch the traffic for an hour to see how malleable the guards were. I wanted to know if they were consistent in keeping out all sentients who didn't belong. Were they bribable or occasionally lax in their duties?

During my wait, I started putting faces to organizations. Each of the great trading houses—of which there were five— had unique armbands on their respective white or black robes. Regardless of which house a representative belonged to, they always entered the north gate area with several guards bearing ornate facial tattoos, each house with its own distinct pattern. Clearly, there was a lot of ink in the city—each visitor had a string of them down their arm—but these tattoos were different from your run-of-the-mill face tattoos. Infiltration was going to take more than an armband and panache; you would need a support staff and passable fake tattoos for that staff.

However, the duke's guards, marked by a playing card on their robes, were allowed entry as individuals, provided they were of a certain rank, based upon a series of armbands. The hierarchy was not immediately discernable, but the pattern was easy to figure out once several junior members were refused entrance while their commanders gained entrance.

My shady spot was rapidly disappearing as it neared eleven o'clock, when four extra gate guards came from within, one of which I recognized as having high rank. A few minutes later, a large motley group led by a member of House Flores and five tattooed adjuncts came up the street. The house member greeted the high-ranking guard and presented a piece of paper from which he called out various names. Each call was answered by one of the unaffiliated crew who then passed through the gates. I marked down the time in my memory storage along with the faces and associations, and headed south.

I stretched my legs and continued methodically exploring Las Vegas, recording street names where available, asking names when I had to, and mentally noting the type and location of each vendor along the way. After an hour and a half, I had the largest trunk streets mapped, but the sun was in full blaze and my stomach rumbled. A man cannot live on coffee and candy alone. I headed back to the hotel to meet the others.

Lunch was a bean and squash soup with more cornbread, and it was as tasty as the prior meals. We'd gotten lucky with the Martinez family. Zew and Diana described the fights as we ate. The early morning fights were criminal bouts or those unlucky enough to roll poorly on the wheel at the gates. Neither of them were impressed by the fighting abilities of those contestants. Amateurs working their way to professional status followed, and during trade season, there were caravan bouts open to all with beast fights interspersed in between.

"Tell him what you told us," Diana prodded Soledad between mouthfuls of cornbread.

"The professionals fight the last fight every Friday, and they allow amateurs to compete if they prove themselves worthy."

"Tell him how much they pay," she continued.

"They pay the day's winner seven eagles. If the second is still alive, they get three."

"That would be an easy way to make money," Zew noted. My hesitation was a statement in-and-of-itself, and the warrior added the caveat, "for me, at least. Diana wouldn't have any problems, either. She'd just keep them from hitting her until she gets to the last fighter, and they'd kill themselves."

"And what would you do if they made you fight each other?" I asked pointedly.

"Don't be stupid, Stonewall," Diana dismissed my concern. "We'd fight as a team."

"Okay, okay. I'm not saying 'no,' but we should wait our two weeks before doing anything like that. And if nothing happens, we can come back the other way and test that route before deciding to risk our lives over some coin," I said cryptically, purposefully omitting reference to the silver sphere in public.

Zew sighed into his bowl. "It's the only way we're going to get out of here," he said fatalistically. Diana nodded in agreement.

"We've got to get on one of the large caravans to get back home. I don't see any other way either," she said.

I hated to agree with them, but I did. "I'd just like to exhaust all the other possibilities before jumping into 'let's just kill them all' territory."

They looked at me, eyed each other, and broke out in laughter. Diana addressed me, "Let me take a guess at how you spent your time while we were enjoying the fights. You scouted out Las Vegas, searching for its weaknesses, and then you started making plans that involved one or more of the following: infiltration, escape, or destruction."

"I also had another cup of coffee," I argued, unable to defend myself against their accusations.

"You talk a lot about how you don't want to do what you spend all your time thinking about doing," Zew stated plainly. "One day, you won't be conflicted about it, or at least you won't feel the need to pretend you're conflicted about it. Not that there's a difference, from where I'm sitting." He stirred the dregs of his soup.

"But you're not wrong," Diana threw in, noticing that they were hitting closer to home than I appreciated. "We'll explore all our avenues before doing what's required."

"Kinda like having a few weeks in the city anyway," Zew concluded, crumbling the remains of the cornbread into his soup.

Chapter Five

Everyone's Got a Plan...

We went our separate ways for the next two weeks, gathering together over breakfast and dinner to discuss what we'd seen or heard. Diana and Zew went to the colosseum every day and spent their time learning about the various fighters, their strengths and weaknesses, when they tended to fight, and when the big fights happened. Soledad shared their enthusiasm for the bouts and informed us about the social clubs associated with each of the major gladiatorial groups and where you could buy small pamphlets containing histories and results. This basic level of knowledge eased their reconnaissance, allowing them to mingle among the spectators and glean additional information regarding the most-current activities.

I spent my time mapping out the city and deciphering the comings and goings at the north ward, which is what the natives called the wall-encircled area that separated the north gate from the rest of Las Vegas. I used a mix of pure observation and playing the bumbling curious tourist to elicit the patterns out of the locals. It's not hard to play the "I'm new in town, what's going on?!" card in Vegas.

Every other day at noon, a large motorized caravan headed north along the old I-15 to the Colorado Kingdoms and returned three days later around six in the morning. They had the rest of the day to recuperate before departing anew the next day. There were two crews that alternated stints, one arriving in the morning with the second crew heading out later that day, so only one convoy was on the road at any given time. Logistically, it minimized exposure and ensured that one troop wouldn't need to pass another on the highway. And I do mean troop—each crew was composed of at least a hundred sentients.

I tried working my way into conversations with the crew, but they were a closed-mouth lot. I quickly got the impression they'd been told to keep their mouths shut and let up with the questions to avoid attracting attention to myself. However, the mission-discipline they displayed wasn't shared by one former crewmember who hung around the same bars they frequented. Of ursine descent, Makwa's entire body was covered in fur and his scraggly lion-like mane was his version of an unkempt beard. He was missing both his legs, lost on his last mission back to Vegas, but he had two working arms which facilitated his predilection for drink. I ruthlessly plied him with free beverages until I finally got him to spill the beans the night before our two weeks ended.

My hirsute drinking companion informed me of the deathlanders haunting I-15 and I-70, the route all the motorized caravans with big rigs were forced to take to get to and from the Colorado Kingdoms. Back in his day, they were unified under a single leader and it wasn't rare for one out of every five caravans to go missing. Nowadays they were broken up into multiple factions, and only one convoy a month goes missing over the seven months the caravans ride. Even with the improved success rate, he wasn't impressed with the quality of the current crews—not like they were when he was riding.

I also learned that once they make it over the Rockies and onto the plains, the caravan splits up into three smaller groups that go to the Boneyard, the Library, or to the Deutschendorfers, a crazy religious clan of "smoke-happy, alcohol-hating vegetarians" that make you listen to the recordings of the Great Denver every day you bunk there. He didn't know much about the Boneyard—it not being around in his day—besides the fact that a wizard known as the Bone Lord was master there, while the Library was ruled by a reclusive wizard who was only interested in books. If you wanted to spend a week there, you had to have a book to trade, no matter how many eagles you offered.

"But what makes the trip so damn dangerous is that yeh can't use guns while you're doing it," Makwa slurred. He was well into his cups.

"The duke won't let you?"

"No, no, no…the duke ain't got nothing against 'em. It's the Lawman that'll get yeh. He's the only one who's got the right to bear arms on that stretch of highway."

My skin goosebumped at the mention of the Lawman. I involuntarily touched the thin bracelet Efte made from her own hair to warn me of danger. Holding a spirit within in, it was enchanted to burst into flame whenever one of the shadow people following me tried to get me killed by moving something of mine.

"The Lawman?"

"Terrible spirit—rides a flaming horse and carries a massive iron gun. Anything he shoots he kills, and he hardly ever misses. Yeh carry a loaded gun through his jurisdiction and he'll send yeh to the grave."

"Well, surely there's a sorcerer around who could take care of him," I said. "The duke's got to have at least a few on his personal staff."

He looked at me and laughed like I'd just swallowed a bug. "Oh, that's rich. Just send a sorcerer in and take care of it! Look, kid, that's the Lawman out there. It ain't some Johnny-come-lately revenant, or inimical chindi, or flighty fortunate son we're talking about—it's the soul of every lawman that ever was and ever will be! It ain't got time for judge and jury, and it knows when you're breaking the rules. There ain't a sorcerer west of the Mississippi that'd dare face it, let alone bring it to flesh and trap it." He drained his mug and slammed it down on the table in emphasis.

"Okay, I get the picture," I placated Makwa; I didn't want him causing a scene and drawing attention to me. "The

Lawman stops all firearm use on the trail and you have to fight it out the old-fashioned way." I waved down the server to refill his drink as I spoke.

"Well, not the whole trail. Yeh got an hour or so outta Vegas before you're in his territory and once yeh hit the mountains west of the Colorado Kingdoms, you're in the clear...but for most of it, yeah." Soothed for the moment, he regaled me with another tale while I mulled over the Lawman.

"Hasn't anyone tried to lure the Lawman from that location so they could use a gun?" I steered him back to what interested me—always seeking to exploit the corner-case.

"Huh?" Makwa was disoriented from my rapid change in subject and his steadily rising blood-alcohol level.

"Say you make a criminal load a gun in his territory just outside Vegas, and then while the Lawman's killing the criminal, the sentients on the caravan load their weapons and take care of the wastelanders real quick-like," I elucidated.

"Won't work. The late duke tried it. The Lawman can be in more than one place at a time," he responded. "Like your style, though. Got any weasel stock in yeh?"

I would have liked to ask him more questions, but the drink I'd just ordered him proved to be his last of the night. He put his thick hairy arms on the table between us, rested his head on them, and gracefully passed out. I tried to rouse him with a shake on his shoulder, but he was having none of it.

When I recounted the conversation at breakfast, taking

time to explain the history of the bracelet Efte made, Diana chimed in, "See, you were always going to be here. No one can avoid their fate."

Zew grumbled in agreement, his mouth full of menudo. "Would have been nice if you'd left us out of it." He looked to be nursing a hangover.

"That's the morning speaking," I quipped. "I suspect you'd have answered differently last night."

He chuckled. "Truth. I shouldn't have bothered going to sleep; I'd probably feel better."

We didn't have time to dawdle—we had to be atop the ruined Phoenix Casino by 9:24 a.m. in order to be there exactly fourteen days after we first touched the orb, and we wanted a ten-minute hedge just to be on the safe side. We quickly finished breakfast and settled our bill with Soledad's parents before returning our rented weapons to Ignacio and recovering our deposit. However, exiting Las Vegas was a more convoluted affair involving customs and a tattoo removal machine for me; Diana and Zew just turned over their steel resister necklaces. The removal hurt a hell of a lot worse than the tattoo. I really want my idea to pan out, if only to avoid repeating the tattoo removal. At least we had our weapons back: I'd missed the comfort of the lethal M1B at my side.

We wormed our way out of the crowds at the south gate and stood upon our landing point with half an hour to spare. The sun was already blazing, proudly displaying its relentless indifference to those below. I gazed upon the city we had grown to know, teasing out its inner workings over the past two weeks. A water caravan heading to Lake Mead threw up a dust cloud east of the city, and the larger structures, once mysterious blocks of settlement, were now known in name and purpose. The same aerial view we had two weeks ago was now enhanced, colored by the context gained from our time there.

The moment neared and we placed our hands upon the silver sphere. "I really hope this works," Zew admitted quietly. I was surprised by his fervent tone; for a guy who said he was convinced we would have to fight our way home, he sounded sincerely willing to be proven wrong.

"3, 2, 1..." I counted down.

Nothing happened.

"Let's give it a few minutes, and then on to Plan B?"

They nodded in agreement and we held on to the sphere until it became obvious there wasn't a return trip coming our way.

"To the duke then." Diana relinquished the defunct sphere, which I placed in my pack.

"How would you prefer to play this: truth, lie, mix?"

"I'd prefer the truth," Zew replied.

"I'd rather hedge our bets a bit and not reveal everything unless we have to," Diana qualified, "but, yeah, generally truth."

"All right, we err on the side of truth, then," I agreed. I was going to be the one doing most of the talking, as I was the most human-looking of us and would be assumed to be the wizard of the inscribed greeting.

We descended the stairs of the Phoenix and approached the city via the southern gate. This time, however, we didn't queue up and aimed straight for the center, pushing our way through the crowd to attract the attention of the gate guards. There were a lot of angry words regarding our actions and things could have gotten heated, but when I pulled out the sphere, the guards blared a horn, instantly hushing the unruly masses. The gate guards, unlike the customs guards, were well-informed regarding the duke's desires.

The highest-ranking guard on duty bowed deeply and addressed me, "Welcome, Great Wizard! Please follow us and we'll take you to the duke." The title "Wizard" scared the crowd, which somehow managed to pull back a good ten feet in all directions, something I would have considered impossible given the press of sentients.

The first thing you need to know about wizards is that they are not synonymous with sorcerers. Sorcerers are humans who see the spirits of the dead—as well as natural or demonic ones—and can transform them into flesh. Sorcerers can kill and harvest said spirits-made-flesh to place them within an object, effectively making it magical, like my hair bracelet or Grendel's flaming sword. Their enchantments are powered by the conquered spirits bound within the items. Sorcerers are unnerving and generally feared due to their ability to communicate with the otherworld, but they're commonly uncommon, meaning that everyone has met one at some time or another.

Wizards, however, are truly rare and extremely powerful and dangerous. Wizards are a union of sorcery and super science; in addition to their sorcerous abilities, they also use, create, and repair technology like tinkers. This mingling of magic and science is ultimately incompatible and unstable, turning wizards—to use the common parlance—batshit crazy. Meteorically crazy. You've got the picture: imagine a nutter with the abilities of Morien and Marilyn wielding magic and a rocket launcher, and you understand why the mob outside the gate backed off.

I've never seen a wizard in person and only know of a few via word of mouth: the Great Kalamazoo, the Saint Cloud, and the aforementioned Bone Lord and Librarian. And no, I'm not thrilled that my way home has a high probability of leading me through one of their territories, but that's the way the cookie crumbles.

The head guard, a skink-descended sentient who introduced himself as Jack Strummer, summoned an escort of ten more guards and we went directly through the gate, ignoring weapons check and customs. Two larger guards beat a course through the crowd as we proceeded, ensuring our way was clear, while another guard ran ahead to notify the duke of our arrival. Strummer remained quiet but attentive as we walked, ready to serve at a moment's notice were he required.

It wasn't long before Strummer delivered us through the gates of the duke's castle and into the hands of the duke's personal guard. They quickly and silently led us into the depths of the compound and eventually into the presence of the duke himself. The duke was a small sentient of orange-throated, side-blotched lizard heritage. Even though he was fully bipedal, he only stood four feet tall. Most sentients don't swing as close to their original stock as the duke—were he not donning a periwinkle crushed-velvet unitard with a silvery belt, I would have easily dismissed him as an usually large lizard if I passed him in the dunes.

A gawky human-looking sentient attended the duke. I assumed he was a sorcerer given his getup: a robe covered in stars and a pointy hat. I think he took the old saying "dress for the job you want" a bit too literally. Long brown locks flowed from under the hat, accentuating how tall and thin his frame was beneath the copious folds of his celestial robe. A second attendant stood on the other side of the duke. Of Gila monster descent and dressed in more practical clothing suited to a workshop, I pegged her as a tinker.

"Greetings, Great Wizard!" the duke began with a curt little bow. "Forgive my intrusion, but my need is great and I intend to provide a generous recompense for your inconvenience." I nearly interrupted, but he barreled forward and I thought it best to let him finish before informing him we weren't who he thought we were.

"Since the fall of mankind, the Lucky Duchy has thrived through trade. The world's goods pass through our gates, and it is through us that the eastern and western parts of this great continent are connected. Against great adversity, we have bloomed in this barren land and set forth the rule of law and civility over the barbarism that once lurked here.

"This is not to say that we are absent problems. For generations, we have traded with the Colorado Kingdoms for the goods of the Central Sea and our trade has profited all involved. But a mighty thorn has vexed us and limited the expanse of civility—the Lawman." The duke paused for dramatic effect. "This powerful spirit makes our trade significantly more difficult, and it is because of this that we seek your unmatched abilities."

Finished with his exposition, I decided it was the right time to speak. I led with a deep bow, which Diana and Zew hurriedly matched and held. "Forgive us, Great Duke, but we are not who you seek." Out of the corner of my bowed eye, I saw the guards fidget at my pronouncement.

"Please continue," the duke permitted, his voice still pleasant but without the persuasive undertones of his prior speech.

"We do not understand what has happened. We found the silvery sphere in the ruins of building recently brought down in a conflict between powers along the western shore of Lake Michigan. When I touched it, it activated and brought us here. I am not a wizard, nor sorcerer or tinker; our apologies for the confusion and disappointment."

"On the *west coast* of Michigan?" the duke asked pointedly.

"Yes, Your Grace," I replied, taking a stab at the proper honorific.

"How did it come there, Gornel? You said it would arrive on the eastern shore," the duke spoke over his shoulder to his tinker.

"I am certain it arrived there properly, Your Grace. I can only assume it was transported somehow," Gornel responded without hesitation.

"If I may be of assistance, Your Grace," I interjected. "The creatures that we fought were vulture men that extorted tribute from the nearby population. It is not unbelievable that they would have received the sphere in that manner."

Gornel shot me a thankful look while the duke provided an entirely different one before addressing her again, "And how did this non-sorcerer trigger the sphere?"

"I am as puzzled as you, Your Grace. The sphere tests the holder's lineage, and there isn't a way to bypass that via trickery." Ever see a Gila monster sweat?

"Again, if I may be of assistance, what do you mean by 'tests the holder's lineage'?"

"The sphere checks the DNA of the holder to ensure it

isn't modified in any way, if you understand such terms," she elaborated.

"Ah, then all is clear. I am a castaway newly arrived in this world. My DNA is as human as those of sorcerers."

"My Lord Duke, his explanation is reasonable," Gornel confirmed. "It appears only through ill chance that the sphere has returned without its intended visitor."

The duke looked toward his comically dressed sorcerer, who nodded his head in agreement.

"Well then, it appears we have three unfortunates who have wasted official materials," the duke decreed. "Given the circumstances, the death penalty would be unjust, but as fate has placed them here, let it cast them into the colosseum for a single bout. If they survive, I'll gift them an eagle. If they don't, they've gifted me their belongings, which are far from the value of the sphere they wasted."

The guards drew to attention, anticipating the duke's final words: "Take them away!"

Chapter Six

...Until They're Punched in the Mouth

"If we would have done things my way, it would have turned out a lot better," Zew said for the millionth time, looking through the bars of the cell we had resided in for the past two days while we waited for our time in the arena. To his credit, it was actually the first time he had said it, but it felt like the millionth time because I had been constantly saying it to myself ever since we were chucked in here with the other six dozen sentients awaiting combat.

Ever since we landed behind bars, I worried that I would have to fight either Zew or Diana, but my worst fear was that they would have to fight each other, which I suspected they'd refuse to do it and then be executed for their defiance. During our stay, several different groups had been called up, and it seemed that those sentenced together fought together, which matched Diana and Zew's observations of the colosseum fights. Hopefully, that would be the same in our case, but the way my luck's been running, I wouldn't be all that surprised if it turned out otherwise.

The daily morning guards arrived and shouted out the

names of those next in line. "Stonewall, Diana, Zew! It's your time to die!" They unlocked the cell and escorted us down a long dank hallway to a large chamber. The dark walls of the chamber were littered with arms and armor. The selection was split into lettered sections and each piece rested upon a numbered peg. Along the far wall was something that looked suspiciously like an old bingo cage. A scarred old gladiator approached us as the guards dropped us off and took position near the two entrances.

"My name is Karas and I've got the next half hour to try to save your life," he opened with a flat bark. "Upon these walls are the weapons and armor you may use to defend yourself. You may choose two of each. But before you choose, his Gamblence Royal Flush had decreed that one of you will trust fate in the choice of arms."

He pointed at me, "You, randomly pull four balls out of the cage and equip yourself with the matching items. The rest of you can choose as you wish, but make it snappy."

Zew and Diana grabbed spears and steel batons for weapons. For armor, Zew selected a metal greave for his left leg and a wooden shield upon which an old stop sign was riveted. Diana opted for a set of football shoulder pads with a rib protector and a matching football helmet, both spray-painted neon orange. Fate was fickle with my choices: I ended up with a good chain hauberk and well-conditioned ring-hilt spatha, coupled with a WWI Pickelhaube and weighed hooked net. I had no clue how to use the net, and was nearly as clueless with the sword—I was an assassin from 2112, after all—but at least my armor was good.

"Now that you have your gear, do any of you need instruction before you head out?" the grizzled fighter inquired.

"A net? What am I supposed to do, catch tuna?" I snarked.

Karas took the net from me and walked away thirty feet. "Draw your weapon and try to kill me," he instructed with a similar inflection of a television chef instructing the viewer to chop onions. I obeyed and came at him, although I did not aim to kill. He spun like a discus thrower and the net flew open, wrapping around my sword arm and head, entangling both together; the hooks were not injurious but grabbed against any surface.

"You are now a tuna, no?" he asked facetiously.

Zew and Diana laughed but helped me out of the net nonetheless. Karas offered instruction to anyone else who needed it, but both of my companions passed. "It's your lives," he shrugged. He left us to ourselves for the remaining time and wandered over to a small table where he took a seat and drank out of a steel canteen.

"You both know I have no idea how to use this sword, right?" I whispered.

"It doesn't matter, Stonewall," Zew confided. "Listen up—we've gotten lucky. The duke isn't as vengeful as he could have been, because the first fight of the day is the weakest.

We two"—he pointed at Diana and himself—"should be able to take care of this without much assistance from you. We're going in bull formation; you stay in the middle behind us like the head of a bull, and Diana and I will be the horns. All you have to do is support us when we reveal vulnerabilities in an opponent. About the sword—if you ever feel the need to get disarmed, I'll do the same so you can re-arm yourself with a spear. Don't worry about me—I'll eventually work my way to your sword. But whatever you do, don't make it obvious or else they'll kill us for cheating." Zew glanced over at Karas to make sure he wasn't eavesdropping but the seasoned fighter took no mind to our huddle. "Considering how poorly you'll perform with that sword, it probably won't be faked."

I found Zew's confidence both reassuring and insulting at the same time.

"Since you're holding the net on your left," Diana continued for him, "I'll be on your left fighting defensively while Zew fights aggressively on your right. Just spin the net around like a shield and the audience will understand you don't have any idea what you're doing. That way, they'll give all their attention to us; we need to get the audience involved immediately to hedge our ruling."

"Ruling?" I asked, instantly regretting the fact that I hadn't attended a single colosseum event.

"The criminals that win their fights are pardoned of their crimes, but they can still be forced to fight again in the next round if the crowd isn't entertained enough with their performance."

"Got it. Put some showmanship into it."

"That's the gist," Zew said as the noise from the crowd crescendoed. "That'll be the end of the animal fight. We're next."

The guards corralled us down another corridor into a brightly lit room that opened to the colosseum via one of the smaller portcullises. My eyes refused to adjust to the light before we were pushed out into the blinding arena, rendering the sky, walls, and sand into a hazy indistinct wash of blue, white, and tan. Diana positioned herself forward and to the left while Zew did the same on my right. Tightly squinting against the glare, I kept my position between them as they advanced toward the shadows on the other end of the sands. I hoped they could see better than I could.

The spectators rumbled we closed the distance. My eyes finally adapted to the light and my vision returned. The indistinct shadows opposite us sharpened into five rough-looking sentients of horned-lizard stock. They were all armed with spears and various smaller backup weapons. Their armor was all over the place.

"Beware their eyes!" I called out to my allies over the roiling noise from the stands. "The lizard they're descended from can shoot blinding blood out of it its eyes!" They both nodded but said nothing, their eyes fierce and mouths stern. Not for the first time, I was glad to be behind them instead of facing them; either one would chew me up and spit me out in hand-to-hand combat with anything other than knives.

Our convergence across the sand seemed to take forever. Time's always a contrary companion indifferent to my desires; it slows and speeds as it wills. As we moved, our opponents adjusted their wedge shape into a horn formation not unlike our own, only wider and enveloping our points within their own. I started spinning my net as advised and the subsequent hubbub from the crowd suggested Diana's strategy was sound; if playing the fool increased my chance of survival, let me put a cap with bells on and I'll be right there.

"Hup Ah!" the lizards yelled and suddenly launched their spears. The interior spears were poorly thrown and fell short, but the spears thrown by those in the horn-position were on target. Zew deftly brushed his away with his shield while Diana dodged and parried with her spear. I broke formation to grab the spear thrown at her, dropping my useless sword and net. At least one problem was solved.

I rejoined the formation and barely heard Zew yell at me over the din, "Now you can actually help us!"

I was about to issue a suitable rejoinder but the lizards released a hissing call, drew their secondary weapons, and charged. Without obvious communication, Zew and Diana traded positions mere seconds before they were upon us. I stepped up between their horns and engaged the middle foe, ensuring they wouldn't face more than two opponents at once.

The lizard in front of me was armed with an aluminum baseball bat and armored with a shield like Zew's and a poorly repaired stab vest. He was short with stubby arms, and I kept him at bay by jabbing my spear point at various locations, learning his reaction speed in the process.

While I tested my opponent, Zew downed one of the interior horn lizards with an artful neck strike. The enemy dropped his weapon and fell to his knees, clutching at his throat with both scaled hands before tipping over into unconsciousness. The second lizard was a stronger combatant, but he must have realized he was outclassed with only a mace. Blood shot out from his eyes as he retreated from the wastelander. Even with forewarning, Zew barely dodged the rapid stream of blood, and that split second was all the lizard man needed to rearm himself with the spear he'd previously thrown.

To my right, Diana had also already downed the interior-horn lizard with a straight thrust through his left eye. Her second opponent was armed with a sword, so I knew she wasn't in any real danger, although she was putting on quite a performance for the crowd.

By now my opponent realized you shouldn't bring a bat to a spear fight, so he tried the same maneuver as his companion to rearm with a more competitive weapon. However, I was faster than Zew and dodged the bloodstream while striking out with my spear. The tip grazed the forearm of the bat-wielder and he couldn't help but drop it. I went in for the kill, but he was adroit with his shield, beating me back until he acquired my dropped net with a sudden leap and roll.

My back to Zew and Diana, he knocked aside another spear thrust with his shield and then whirled and spun the net as Karas had done minutes before. I dropped to a knee and twisted to the right, dodging the flying net. I silently thanked the old gladiator for not tolerating my mouthiness. He'd said it was his job to save my life, and that's what he'd done.

Two nearby screams announced the end of the foes facing Diana and Zew, shortly followed by a swift spear flying over my shoulder. The spear went through the shield of my opponent and came to rest deep within his chest. A fountain of blood sprayed out of his upturned mouth and he violently expired on the stained sand.

The stands took to their feet, roaring in approval as Diana and Zew pumped their arms over their heads. I didn't immediately join with them; it didn't feel much like a reason to celebrate. Who knew what potentially ridiculous crime this group of dead lizard men had committed? Diana shot me a look that made me reconsider, and I tiredly aped their crowd-appeasing behavior.

The gate that brought us into the arena rose behind us and two groups of guards rushed out: one to drag the dead bodies away, one to escort us back into the depths of the colosseum. The gate closed behind us while another opened elsewhere, starting another contest. No need to make the bloodthirsty wait any longer than absolutely necessary, after all, and a heavy docket of criminals reduced the time available between fights.

While we removed our armor, the highest-ranking escort guard approached us, handing us an eagle. "You're free to go. Your crimes against the duke have been paid." He motioned to another guard. "Carlos will show you the way out. Here are your customs' receipts; don't lose them."

He handed us our papers and Carlos took off at a brisk pace. We followed him through a maze of long curved corridors and interlocking rooms. He deposited us among the milling throng of spectators on the concourse without a single word. Diana smiled as he left and grabbed Zew's arm. "Let's get a drink and watch the rest of the fights!"

Chapter Seven

Plan C

I left them to their amusements and wandered back to Hotel White House. Soledad's parents were surprised to see me, but welcomed me back with open arms when I booked and prepaid rooms for myself and Zew and Diana for the next month. I figured they'd saved my butt in the ring, so it's the least I could do. I knew what was coming next, and a little good will from them would go a long way.

I was quietly eating some tamales when Soledad passed through the hotel lobby that adjoined the restaurant. She happily bounced up to me and actually gave me a little hug.

"I thought you'd left!"

"I got arrested and had to fight in the arena," I told her. No point in lying to the kid. She lived in a rough world and had no doubt seen worse.

She looked me up and down. "Well, at least you're not dead or injured."

I raised my mug of beer in her direction. "It certainly could have been worse."

Although we'd only employed her to show us around the

city for four days, she'd always been around while we were here, and in the evenings she played guitar and sang on a stool in the corner of the restaurant. She was pretty good and we threw in some change every once in a while to promote her hustle. She hung around hoping for more interaction, but I wasn't my normal jovial self so she eventually skittered away to tout up more business.

I spent the rest of the day drinking and was well-past tipsy by the time Zew and Diana returned. They sat down at my table with an air of anticipation about them; I assumed it was either a lecture or a giant "I told you so," but I was too far into my cups to mind. An exchange of looks assessed my condition and that tomorrow would be a better time for the speech they'd prepared; they ordered some food instead.

"It's all right, you know," I slurred.

Diana raised her eyebrows.

"I mean, I know what I need to do, and believe it or not, it doesn't really bother me that much. I'm not conflicted." I directed the comment to Zew. "It's just the...the *final surrender*, you know? I've manage to keep myself apart from this"—I gestured around me—"but now, I'm not going to be able to do that anymore. I have to go native."

I paused for another gulp and saw the confusion on their faces. "See? You don't even know what that means! That's what I'm talking about." I slammed my mug a little more forcefully than I had intended and a little beer sloshed over the lip. "I can't stay in two times; I have to choose. And *this* time is the one that's being chosen." I tapped my index finger pointedly on the table for emphasis.

"I can't go back and I can't walk away; you rely on me. Maybe not as much as I do on you, I admit, but you know, you do. At least some. I've just got the feeling that things are going to get weirder before they get normal again. Whatever the hell normal is." I said a lot of progressively more obscure and convoluted stuff before they eventually carried me up to my bed. I immediately passed out and enjoyed a dream-free night.

People born under the shattered moon call this "Castaway Sickness," their catch-all term for the troubles those of us out-of-time go through while adapting to our new circumstances. It's a simplistic term for a complex and evolving situation, but it provides an escape valve for those of us living through it: it allows natives to classify and accept strange behavior as something sporadic and cleansing rather than permanent and dangerous.

I woke late the next morning and found them waiting for me at breakfast. I sat down and was about to order when a steaming plate of chilaquiles with a side of nopalitos was brought to me.

"We ordered for you," Diana explained.

"We've got to be at the training yard in an hour, so eat up," Zew advised.

I dove in, ready to hear about their plans. Feeding me mouthful after mouthful of delicious beans, cheese, and cactus wasn't a bad way to butter me up for bad news.

"We've hired Karas to train us for the gladiatorial matches," Diana started. "The last caravan heads out in a little over two months and the selection process for new guards is a series of at least four increasingly-difficult bouts, more if there are a lot of contenders. This gives us a month to learn how to fight as best as possible. Each session is four hours long."

"You two don't need instruction," I posited.

"For our chosen weapons, no," Zew agreed. "But the final battle is a randomized trial; chance will assign us weapons and armor via the balls in the rotating cage, as it did for you yesterday."

"It was an old Bingo cage," I corrected him instinctively. "Never mind—not important."

"Karas will instruct us in the use of all the possible weapons," he continued. "There are sixty different weapons in the pool. We'll get about two hours on each one during our four weeks with him. It's not a lot of time, but you know better than any of us how even a minute can be enough to save your life. There will also be some overlap between the weapons, so it sounds worse than it is."

Zew hesitated before proceeding, something I had never seen him do before. "We know you're not interested in watching the fights but you need to get over it. It's too dangerous for you not to have a basic knowledge of how everything works and how the more-experienced gladiators conduct themselves in the ring."

"You don't have to go to the morning contests, but you're going to have to at least go to the evening ones to watch the professionals," Diana added.

I wolfed down the last of my breakfast and said, "You've convinced me. Let's get this done and get out of here. Lead the way."

They both looked genuinely surprised by my lack of pushback—it's enough to convince a guy he's got a reputation for being contrary. They hid their astonishment quickly and we arrived at the training yard half an hour later. On the way, Diana gave me a red metal pass; it was about the size of a credit card with multiple rectangles stamped out of it like an old punch card. The facility was hidden behind an adobe wall twice my height and accessible through a single gate. We presented our passes at the gate and the guards motioned us to a full-body turnstile. I took the lead and swiped my card into the slot at the hub until it buzzed, indicating it was now unlocked. Once I went through, it immediately locked again. Diana and Zew followed me, amused by the novelty of the process.

They swiftly collected themselves as we entered a massive arcaded exercise yard; several hundred gladiators were practicing either against each other or their instructors. For the true beginners, there were thick metals poles driven into the earth, encircled by heavy hempen rope. Two smaller courtyards branched off the main area and Zew lead us to the northern one. A sign over the entrance read: "Caravan Gladiators Only; Red Passes Required."

There wasn't a guard so we let ourselves in, picking out Karas across a field full of gladiators. Surrounded by six or seven attendants and piles of equipment, he rested on a bench in the shade beneath the bright green awnings that ran the length of the arcade. We waved to get his attention, and by the time we arrived, his assistants—one which had the look of a former gladiator himself—had everything set up.

We barely had time to set aside our spears when he started. "First up is the queen of all weapons: the spear!" He tossed us blunt spears and grabbed one for himself. "Whichever of you is weaker with the weapon will face me first," he said, moving into the yard.

I took a step forward but Zew interjected, "We don't need spear practice. We're well versed in it. I'm an instructor."

Karas turned around, "I'll be the judge of that. You first, then!"

Zew entered the field and they tipped points in respect before starting. They faced off, tips barely moving in a subtle challenge to each other, but within moments Karas burst out with a rough laugh, "All right, that's enough! I trust your judgment—you don't need training with a spear."

He threw his spear to the ground for his servants to pick

up, held out his right hand, and called out, "Spatha! The weakest among you three, arm and at me!" One of the servants delivered the blunted weapon to the seasoned fighter along with a small buckler shield while three others equipped us with a similar pairing.

Once I geared up, I entered to meet him, turning the point of the spatha to the ground before squaring off. He held the buckler nearly arm's length in front of him and circled to my right. I followed his track and blocked his first attack with my buckler. He backed up and then followed through with a series of strikes, testing my reflexes by varying the angle of attack. After half a minute, he got down to business and hit me with a series of blows that ended with what would have been a killing strike.

"Good reaction time, but no experience with this weapon or shield," he assessed, half statement, half question.

"Yes," I responded. "I'm faster and stronger than I look, but unlike those two, I lack experience."

He nodded and pointed to his gladiator attendant. "You'll train with my old friend Zuma. He'll work you through the proper movements of each weapon, the stances and attack angles. You need more work than I'll be able to provide, and my skills would be better used improving your companions."

"Next!" he called out and Diana stepped up. As they sparred, Zuma and I stepped away for my practice. He was one of the many Gila-stock sentients in Vegas, fully bipedal with distinct black and corral patterns on his exposed skin and bead-like scales on his short snout. He quickly went through a series of moves and ordered me to repeat them. I mimicked the routine perfectly on the first go, and Zuma did little to mask his bewilderment. I'm pretty sure he's never had a student with a computer in his head before.

"Once I'm shown something, I remember it," I explained. "I don't forget."

"That will make this much easier," he replied in a thickly accented, guttural voice. "Okay, how about you try this one." He began another series of buckler and spatha training routines with lithe precision. I watched and repeated what he did, as he did.

He let out a smiling hiss of enjoyment and I saw part of his tongue was gone. "You are the best learner I've ever seen!"

Zuma's praise drew Karas's attention and he backed away from Diana for a second. "What's that?"

"Come here, Karas, and watch the one who learns like a parrot!"

Karas walked over and Zuma made me show him the last routine he'd taught me. He old warrior laughed and clapped me on the back. "Then you will have a chance, after all!" He addressed Zuma, "Work him through all of the routines as soon as possible. He needs time on the field to refine and use what he mimics so quickly."

Zuma nodded and the rest of our time was spent going

through as many weapon combinations as possible, teaching me the basics of each. "We'll get you on the field as quickly as we can once we've gone through all the weapons, and then we'll see just how much you can really remember," he summed up as we parted ways after the session.

Diana and Zew animatedly talked about their session as we walked out of the training area and punched our way through the exit turnstile. Their general consensus was that Karas had been a good choice. "If you get good enough, maybe he'll spar with you before it's over," Diana posited encouragingly, as if getting thwacked by a master was somehow better than getting thwacked by someone a bit less skilled.

"May I be so blessed," I sighed.

Chapter Eight

The ZZZ Society

The next few days were a blur as I focused on my combat studies. I could easily repeat what I'd seen, but using that information during a bout was more difficult. That involved non-cognitive functions, which meant I had to train my muscle memory based around the routines, and the only way to do that is repetition.

To avoid the heat, we started training early and ended mid-morning. We usually stayed for another hour, practicing against each other, before grabbing lunch at the hotel restaurant. After eating, we'd head out to the colosseum and watch the advanced amateurs and caravan bouts until dinner, when we'd return and have the evenings to ourselves to do whatever we wished. I sat between Diana and Zew during the matches, and they kept up a constant patter regarding the battles, slowly indoctrinating me into the world of hand-to-hand combat with ancient weapons.

A week into this routine, I noticed a daily lunchtime visitor in the restaurant. She was a near-human, perhaps with a bit of coyote stock in her. She sat in the corner with her back against the wall, and read a book before and after her meal. There were others who took daily meals there, but they were almost always residents in the hotel and she wasn't, according to Soledad. I also pumped Xavier—the cook and one of Soledad's uncles—for any information on the mystery diner, but he couldn't shed any light except that she said she liked the food.

Two days after I first observed her, she showed up for dinner, something which she had never done before. "May I join you?" Her voice was pleasantly modulated and locally accented.

"If you're paying for beer, I'm listening," I proposed. Although I'd never been a freelancer, her approach had all the signals of a job offer, and I might as well get her to pay for something even if I declined. She went to the bar, brought back two beers, and sat opposite me.

"It's come to my attention that you're someone who can get things done."

I held out my hand. "Hello, my name's William Stonewall. And you would be...?"

She shook my hand. "My name is Tucson."

She had a good poker face, I'd give that to her, "All right, Tucson, what bee's buzzing up your bonnet?"

"As I said, it's—"

"From whom? Who brought it to your attention?"

I could see her waver as she opened her mouth to answer one way and closed it before speaking. I got the feeling she wasn't very experienced with this sort of thing. She took a swallow of beer, no doubt to buy her a little time to think. Her piercing eyes examined me over her mug, sizing me up.

"I'm a representative of the ZZZ."

"That doesn't mean anything to me," I lied. "I'm a castaway."

"The ZZZ is an organization that gathers information for the safety of travelers. You may recognize us from our literature." She dug out a folded pamphlet from her bag and passed it across the table. The typeset words "Twelve Desert Dangers You Won't Believe!" were emblazoned in block print above a poorly drawn snake-like creature that served as a cover image. The booklet detailed twelve creatures, of which I had only seen one: the common lizard-turtle hybrid used as a pack animal. They were called turzards and apparently could spit a burning poison when agitated.

"Looks like a useful public service," I said blandly, tossing the handout on the table after a quick flip through. No need to keep it—once I've seen anything, I remembered it. She conspicuously left it on the table.

"We have hundreds of such publications throughout North America. We're the most-trusted source of information in the new world, and we're—"

"Enough with the advertising. What do you need?"

"One of our members hasn't reported back to us for several weeks and we've been unable to contact him to see if anything's gone wrong."

"Well, if it's been several weeks, something *has* gone wrong.

Professional opinion."

"That's what we suspect as well, and where you and your unique abilities come into play."

"You still haven't told me who brought me to your attention." I took a long drink, waiting for the answer she was hesitant to give.

"Abigail."

I don't know what response she expected, but silence wasn't it. I watched every muscle of her face, every nuance of body language she put forth.

"Abigail," she repeated after an uncomfortable ten seconds.

"I heard you the first time. Why should I believe it?"

"Because it's the truth."

I ran a quick search on my recordings of the conversations I'd had with Zew and Diana since our arrival in Las Vegas. The word "Abigail" appeared six times. She could have overheard a conversation.

"You're going to have to give me more than that if you want me to believe you."

"What could I offer that would convince you?"

"If you've heard of me through Abigail, that means you can communicate with her. Send her a message and get a response. If it checks out, I'll listen to what you have to say."

"That's going to be difficult," she said, wringing her hands.

"Life's hard."

"I can do it, but it's going to take at least a week and there's someone's life on the line while we dither away with this unnecessary authentication process."

"Yeah, but it's also my life on the line. Isn't it?"

"The mission shouldn't be life threatening." Her eyes said differently.

"That's what I thought. Here's my message: 'What's my real name?' You know where to find me when you get a response. I'm going to go upstairs and wait for my friends." I rose from the table, took my mug back to the bar, and went to my room. I peered out my window, waiting for her to leave. Once I spotted her, I jumped out—my room is on the second floor—and tailed her. I don't like working with unknown sentients, and I certainly don't like being the person in the room with the least amount of leverage on everyone else. I trailed her for more than a dozen blocks until she entered a temple dedicated to the Order of the Sun. They were one of the many religions beneath the shattered moon, and only adherents were allowed entrance into their buildings.

At least I'd learned one thing: she wasn't a professional or even an aspiring amateur, as she never thought to check for a tail after leaving Hotel White House. That was consistent with the persona she'd presented to me at the table, so either she was a real professional who occupied her legend at all times or she was as she appeared to be. I favored the latter.

I doubled back to the hotel and waited for Diana and Zew to return. When they entered, I pulled them over to the corner table I'd claimed and told them about what had happened, and how we were waiting for contact from Abigail. Both were speechless.

"You know how I have a computer in my head, right?" I reminded Diana of the conversation we'd had on our way to guard the skies during the raid on the mall rats.

"Yeah, you hear bug voices on it."

Sometimes I swear she pretends to be simple just to get on my nerves. Catching the smallest of smiles cracking out of the corner of her mouth confirmed my suspicion.

I grinned in return. "Basically, yes. It also allows me to remember things really well."

"So *that's* how you can learn the combat routines so quickly," Zew exclaimed. I couldn't be sure what bothered him more—the hardware in my brain or how quickly I was improving under someone else's tutelage.

"Part of it, yes. It also allows me to remember things like how many times one of us has said Abigail's name since we've arrived in Las Vegas. We've said it a total of six times, so it's possible she spied on us, but unlikely."

"If she gets back to you with the right answer, we'll know regardless," Diana remarked neutrally. Neither she nor Zew asked what the message was, nor did I offer, and I appreciated her diplomacy despite her undeniable curiosity.

I nodded. "Hence, the wait."

"What do you think the ZZZ wants?" Diana asked,

directing the question more toward Zew than me.

"It's always information," he stated plainly. "That's really all they do, collect information. Their pamphlets"—he pointed to the one Tucson had left on the other table, which Xavier had added to the guest reading collection—"are just a pretense; it provides them cover for their behavior if they're ever exposed. We won't know what information they want in this situation until she comes back."

"Do you think there's a connection to the Order of the Sun?" I speculated.

"There's got to be some sort of connection, but how much?" He shrugged his well-defined shoulders.

"I could always stake out the place, check up on the incoming and outgoing crowds."

"That would cut into your weapons practice and—what did you call it—'oppositional intelligence' at the colosseum," Diana objected. "That's more important right now. We don't even know if she's legit or what she wants."

Reluctantly, I had to agree that she was right. "Fine, I'll leave it be for now."

Tucson might be a black box at the moment, but the exchange shed more light on the Diana-Zew dynamic. Ever since we'd landed in the Lucky Duchy, they always seemed in sync before approaching me with their plans or thoughts, but Diana had looked genuinely surprised by the whole "I'm a hundred years old" bombshell and Zew didn't know about my computer until tonight. They may be bunkmates and definitely had a lot in common, but they didn't necessarily tell each other everything. Good to know.

Chapter Nine

A Voice from the Distance

The next week was temporally ambivalent: everything was racing like a rabbit or crawling like a turtle. Practice zoomed by and Zew was impressed by the speed of my progress, computer or not. As we trained on a multitude of gladiatorial weapons, he was also learning how to teach better by being a student of a masterful instructor. My two compatriots were pleased with our progression and believed we had a good chance at winning a slot as caravan guards before the season closed.

Initially, I was more worried—in my line of work, a mission has already gone pear-shaped if the bar is set at being the last man standing. Fortunately, only the first three rounds of the battle for caravan positions were lethal affairs, mostly to deter the casual entrants. After that, they were technical bouts with painted weapons that only left marks behind. After all, the duke didn't want to slaughter the best competitors and reduce the selection pool for the next contests. That cheered me right up—I just had to not die for three rounds, much better odds than last man standing.

The mysterious ZZZ agent finally reappeared eight days

after her initial approach. I was eating dinner alone and she sat down opposite me without asking my opinion on the matter. She didn't even offer to pay for the beer I was drinking.

"Nice to see you again, Agent Six."

Well, that answered that question. The only sentients in this time that knew my real name were 1,800 miles away, and although she could be tricking me via a contact in the elder council and not Abigail herself, I was fine with that level of confirmation. There wasn't an elder council member I didn't trust, even if I didn't always see eye-to-eye with all of them.

"And you are? Don't tell me your name is really Tucson."

She gave me a wolfish smile. "You can call me Emily."

"Nice to see you again, Emily. What's the offer?"

"Three weeks ago, a member of the ZZZ failed to file his monthly report. We want you to find out what's happened to him."

"Sounds simple," I snarked. "More information, please."

"The agent's name is Eduardo Ramirez. He's the director at the crematory. He runs all the computers and robotic assistants, ensuring that the processing of dead sentients is uninterrupted."

"Tinker?"

"Yes. The crematory is his domain; the duke only hauls the corpses there and hauls the ash away; everything else is done by Ramirez and his robots."

"So the only way in is in the back of a truck filled with dead bodies?"

"We expect you to find some other method of entrance, but yes, that is one option."

"What's so valuable about the information Ramirez is feeding you?"

"It's demographics information. It helps us keep a finger on the pulse of Las Vegas."

She didn't offer more, so I waited in silence for the real reason. Demographics information, although useful, wasn't something you'd hire me to protect.

"And recently, many members of the various secret societies have been dying at higher-than-normal rates. Ramirez had been reporting on that."

There it was. Now that was something worth keeping tabs on. If someone was waging a covert war against your people or your competitors, you would take risks to uncover all the actors.

"So the mission is break into the crematory, locate Ramirez, or what's left of him, and report back?"

"Yes."

I finished my beer and pushed the empty mug her way. She took my hint and got me another and one for herself as well. I wondered if she was paying or if the ZZZ was footing the bill.

"There's more to it. You could hire someone local for that. There's got to be dozens here that could fill the bill." I sucked down the foam on top of the sub-standard pour.

"You not being local is one of your strong points. Locals

could talk; you're planning to leave soon."

She may not be a professional, but at least she did her homework.

"Expected obstacles? Security systems, guards?"

"As far as we know…" she began, which triggered me a bit. That's not the kind of thing you want to hear come out of a handler's mouth; it made me think that perhaps the relationship between the ZZZ and Ramirez may not be precisely as described. "…there aren't any security systems in place and the only other inhabitants of the crematory are the robots that Ramirez uses for labor."

I nodded and took another drink. "Brass tacks time: payment?"

"We know you intend to return to Deeplac. We can help with that process. If you can make your way to the Library, we can provide a full month's room and board, as well as access to the resources there. In addition, we can provide safe transport through the slave fields of the Colorado Kingdoms and a ship to carry you to Great Suomi."

It wasn't a bad offer, but it put us in a tight situation: everything offered was to be delivered after the service was provided. There'd be little recourse were they to change the terms of the deal. I needed more sugar than that.

"I'd also need ten eagles, as well as ten each for my companions. Paid before I take the mission, so regardless of the outcome, we're not left trusting you to follow through with your promises."

I could tell that thirty eagles was a lot to ask for and her response was predictable. "I'll have to get that approved before I can commit."

"That's okay, I haven't accepted yet either. I want a day to think about it—a day to wander around the target and assess my options."

"Tomorrow at dinner, then?" She reached out her hand to shake on it.

"Tomorrow," I agreed and accepted her hand.

I waited until she left before bolting to follow her again. As before, I lost her trail when she entered the temple of the Order of the Sun. I expected as much, but confirmation was nice. I returned to the restaurant, grabbed another beer, and waited for my scaled comrades. They arrived later than normal, having given the restaurant a wide berth during dinnertime all week in case Emily, née Tucson returned. I hailed them into the restaurant from the hotel lobby.

"She came back?" Diana asked.

"Yep, she's the real thing." I left out the exact call and response to Abigail. They only knew William Stonewall and there was no need for them to meet Agent Six.

"What do they want you to do?"

"I'm supposed to infiltrate the crematory, find out if some guy named Ramirez is still alive, and let them know what's going on."

"Seems simple enough, right up your alley as well," Zew observed. "What's the payment?"

"A month's room and board in the Library, access to said Library, and safe passage to Great Suomi across the Central Sea. I asked for some eagles as well; we'll see how they respond."

"That's a big payout for something that sounds so simple," Diana expressed her suspicion.

"My thoughts exactly."

"It's a good return, though," Zew noted. "Getting across the sea on a chartered boat would greatly simplify matters. How long do you think you'd need to do this? How much would it cut into your lessons and gladiatorial observation?"

"It honestly sounds like a one-night gig. I'd need to scout the location beforehand, but it shouldn't interfere with anything for more than three days—four, tops."

Diana looked at Zew, assessing his opinion on the matter, before speaking for them both. "Anything we can to do help?"

"If you two wouldn't mind being lookouts and a potential distraction while I'm on the mission…"

She grinned a wide smile. "We could work something out."

Chapter Ten

Vegas Life

True to my word, I started scouting out the crematorium to see what I would be getting myself into should I take the gig. Ideally, I would have three or four rounds of recon before settling on a plan, but I'd have a better idea of how much I really needed to scout after the first round. Sometimes things are straightforward, but most of time, they're not.

For only the second time since our arrival, I haunted the streets of Las Vegas after dark, strolling under dim electric lights gleaming white and tan, a far cry from the vibrant neon spectacle it used to be. Even when I was running missions as Agent Six, I'd never been a fan of the nightlife. People do stupid things when the sun is down, and I prefer to operate with the least amount of baseline stupidity as possible. My life is dangerous enough without jackholes mucking things up with their foolishness.

The more rewarding aspect of Vegas at night was the precipitous drop in temperature. It was still warm—there was too much concrete and adobe for it to get as cold at night as it did in the desert proper—but far from the oven of the daytime. This made early night the second busiest time of the day for most sentients, with early morning the most active. Everywhere I went, crowds were milling and moving, tidying up the day's business before bunking down on their woven rope beds topped with the thinnest of mattresses and sheets.

If early morning was for revving up the day, evening was for unwinding, and music ruled the night in Vegas. Entire bands hustled through the streets to make their gigs, and the city swayed to the voiceless hum of every sort of instrument imaginable. Traditional Mexican styles were the strongest influences, but given the nomadic nature of the sentients populating Las Vegas, all manner of music wafted through the air.

I wended my way through the throng and settled opposite the crematory. Thanks to Marilyn's silvery gloves, I shouldn't have a problem climbing it, but there wasn't any place I could go to get eyes on the top of the platform; at ninety feet tall, the first level of the half-scale Eiffel Tower replica was the tallest building in the city. I had nothing more to go on than what I'd seen from the thirty-sixth floor of the ruined Phoenix Casino. From that vantage, the crematory was a two-story steel-then-adobe construction with a circular array of mirrors in a center courtyard.

One of its massive legs jutted toward the street and I perambulated, checking for corrosion. There were minor spots but the arid desert climate was kind to metal—no need to worry about a beam end snapping off when I put my weight on it. I worked my way around the circumference of the tower, inspected the other three legs and reached the same conclusion. The distribution of nearby buildings flagged the southwest leg as the easiest access; it was surrounded by two warehouses and a green grocer that would be closed by the time I moved out.

The area beneath the crematory was clear of structures, acting like a park of sorts despite the fact that corpse processing lay dead center. I had never witnessed cadaver intake, but I suspected they simply loaded them onto the platform of the skeletonized elevator and sent them up into the robots' domain. Adjacent to the elevator shaft was the ash chute, high enough for a vehicle to drive underneath for rapid collection. I kept my distance as I surveilled and feigned mild drunkenness; no need to give anyone the notion I was interested in the crematory.

As I stumbled about, a group of young sentients approached me, the eldest saying, "Hey mister, looks like you've had a little too much to drink. Why don't you let us help you home?"

I straightened up, cold-eyed the speaker, and nodded toward the elevator, "At least they won't have to carry your corpse very far." I drew my knife from its sheath to clarify any possible confusion.

He put up his hands in a conciliatory manner. "Hey, hey, there! Calm down, old friend." But as he spoke, his companions began encircling me.

"They stop now or you die first."

The underlings stopped, which I took as a good sign. The crew was waiting for instruction from their leader in light of a new threat, decreasing the likelihood that any were going to go rogue and attack. Hopefully all of us would walk away without me having to kill anyone.

"No need to go crazy, old man. What the hell's wrong with you?" he said, backing up. His accomplices followed suit. I didn't say anything and waited for them to leave before sheathing my knife. This was what I was talking about—people do stupid things in the dark and I have to deal with them.

The standoff didn't draw much attention, and once they were gone, everyone went about their business as normal. I left the park after the incident, taking care to walk near the elevator so I could see up the shaft to the bottom of the elevator carriage far above. No entry point there—the carriage blocked off access, as there was only a few inches of space between it and the bottom floor of the crematory.

On the way back to Hotel White House, I detoured past the Order of the Sun's temple frequented by Emily. A pair of guards stood outside the door and there was no light cast from within, both of which raised my suspicion. Something about this setup rubbed me the wrong way. Wealthy temples may require extra protection, but religious spaces typically had an inner sanctum where things of monetary or spiritual value were stored and external spaces for the unwashed masses to worship. If something needed to be protected from theft, the guards would be *inside* the temple. There was no need for guards outside of the temple except to act as glorified bouncers for the more exclusive religions, and there were not a lot of devotees of the Sun milling around in the middle of the night.

Hoping to find a rear entrance, I circled around the block, but buildings lined the street the entire way. Either there wasn't a back entrance to the Order of the Sun, or there was a courtyard of some fashion. One of the storefronts close to the back of the temple was a restaurant, currently closed but now a prime destination for tomorrow's lunch. It looked like it had a back patio I could exploit for access to the block's shared courtyard.

I changed my mind and decided to do another pass through the park under the crematory before actually heading back to the hotel. Things had quieted down a bit and in another hour or two, it should be dead, granting me access with little chance of being observed.

Bordora, the Hotel White House's night clerk, was the only one awake when I finally returned. She was of Gila background and was well known for having a poisonous bite, unlike most sentients that shared her heritage. It was probably hell on her love life, but it made her one of the best night clerks—only an idiot would mess with her.

Back in my room, I stared at the ceiling, not quite ready to fall asleep. I couldn't stop thinking about my life. In some ways, the trip to Las Vegas mimicked my trip to the world beneath the shattered moon—both were against my will and both were disruptions from an accustomed life. However, their differences were stark; I understood how I got to Las Vegas and I had a plan to return to Deeplac. I still had no idea how I'd gotten beneath the shattered moon and not even an embryonic idea of how to return to my time. More importantly, I wasn't sure I wanted to return. I'd been through too much to find the life of an assassin for the wealthy and powerful satisfying.

The morning came sooner than I wished and I had to hustle to get to practice on time—Karas wasn't the kind who tolerated tardiness, and I didn't want to irritate someone whom we paid to beat the crap out of us. I arrived with only minutes to spare and geared up for my first all-session spar with Zuma. Spending a little over an hour on each of the sixty weapons used in the arena, I'd finally finished learning all of the attack and defense routines yesterday and demonstrated competency on all of them.

It is a bit of an understatement to say I am an impossibly quick learner thanks to my computer augmentation. I can make the leap from novice to journeyman in just about any field within a week of study, but that's where my big advantage ends—moving from intermediate to higher levels can take me as long as anyone else. Okay, not just anyone, but someone who's got an aptitude for the subject and a desire to learn. If I want to advance to mastery faster than your average journeyman, I need to jack in and be programmed to do so—that's how I obtained twenty-seven different Doctorate-level educations. I wish there was a gladiator-training program I could download instead of dancing around under a relentless sun getting thwacked by fighters who'd been doing it for decades. They enjoyed making me squirm and suffer, and while I understood the psychology behind it—if they could get under my skin and involve my emotions, the lessons would stick better through positive and negative reinforcement—it was little comfort to my bruises and aches. My faster healing rate helped, but it couldn't keep up when I was subjecting myself to daily abuse. I mean training, of course, daily training.

We started out with buckler and spatha, and I managed a killing blow on Zuma in the very first exchange. This stunned everyone, myself more than anyone else.

"You're getting slow, Zuma!" Karas roared with laughter.

"You'll spar with him soon enough, so you may want to watch your mouth, old man! He's as fast as a snake and half as personable," Zuma retorted.

"Tuna not so tuna now, eh?" Karas ribbed me. From the tone of his voice, I feared I'd just gained a nickname.

The rest of the session was particularly rough on the old bones as Zuma was relentless from that point forth. I never got close to hitting him again, as we spun through the various weapon and armor combinations. At the end, I thanked him for his instruction and limped to lunch.

Diana and Zew were battered and bruised as well, but both

of them were such stoics you couldn't tell. Fortunately, I did enough complaining for the three of us.

"You should be more thankful for the training," Diana chided me after one of my longer and more colorful rants.

"Oh, I am. I know they're working me hard to try to keep me alive, but their very existence is terrifying. Intellectually, I know the practice weapons are blunted but my monkey mind knows that if I met either of these two on the sands with real weapons, they'd roll me over like a hog for slaughter. Hell, if I met either of you two in any situation other than a knife fight, it would be the same."

That got Zew's attention, "Knife?"

"Yeah, I'm just about the best knife fighter you'll find," I responded modestly.

"We should test that out someday," he mused. "If you're that good, we could train each other."

"You shouldn't worry about meeting anyone like them on the sands," Diana assured me. "Zuma was a three-time champion before he retired fifteen years ago and Karas was an eight-time champion twenty years ago. Both of them fought in the professional bouts."

My jaw dropped. The chances of being a multi-year champion in a series of lethal fights were slim, while an eight-time champion was infinitesimal. "How the hell did you convince them to train us?"

"They led a revolt against the duke eight years ago and

failed. They were too popular for him to kill, so he confiscated almost all their wealth and made them spend time in menial positions in the arena. They both need money so we provided it, twelve eagles worth."

"That's most of what you had!" I protested.

"Well, isn't it nice to know your friends want to keep you alive?" she teased as she punched me in the arm.

"Yes, it is. Thank you," I responded with genuine gratitude. I was roughly two-thirds of the way through training and if I had to enter the arena on the wrong side of the gate today, I would now stand a decent chance against an amateur regardless of the weapon and armor combination. "How about I buy you two lunch today? There's a new place I want to try out."

"I could eat," Diana said and shrugged while Zew grunted an affirmative.

I led them to the restaurant behind the Order of the Sun's temple and asked for patio seating. The waiter was confused but eventually figured out what I wanted. I guess "patio" isn't a common word anymore, which seems strange given its Spanish roots. You run into these little idiosyncrasies every once in a while under the shattered moon.

The restaurant specialized in sausages, many of which were reptilian-based with an equal number that referenced creatures I'd never heard of before. Zew was thrilled by the menu and happily ordered for us all, explaining the different sausages and which condiments you paired them with. Who knew Zew was a sausage aficionado? Given how many times Diana laughed and touched his arm during lunch, I guessed this aspect of Zew was new to her as well. The warrior spoke more words during that meal than I had heard him speak the first six months in Deeplac. His enthusiasm and vast wurst knowledge provided me ample quality time to surveil the back of the Order of the Sun's temple as he hogged the conversation.

The temple was three stories tall, made of a mix of steel, wood, adobe, and brick. A strong metal door provided access to the shared courtyard, the lintel forming a slight lip above the door. Unlike the barefaced front, the back of the building had four windows—two on each of the upper floors—and all of them had heavy exterior bars. It was secure against intrusion, but the protrusion from the back door was a security flaw—I could pull my way up to the ledge, and then leapfrog and climb my way to the roof via the bars on the windows. The roof may have an exploitable point of entry; it wasn't visible from the thirty-sixth floor of the Phoenix Casino, so I didn't know.

As I cased the joint, I noticed the slightest metal rod over the lip of the third floor. It looked like an antenna, but it was gone the moment I spotted it. Someone was doing something interesting up there, and I definitely needed to get on that roof! If they had an antenna, they might have a ham, shortwave, or citizens' band radio transmitter...I'd love to get my hands on any of them. A radio certainly would explain how the ZZZ was communicating within their organization.

Our sausages came and we dug in under the careful guidance of Zew. I have to admit, he really knew his "flavor profiles" and "complementary spices blends." I didn't even give him a hard time when he insisted on using a palette cleanser between sausages. It was a part of him I'd never seen that bordered on artistic. If he wasn't yanking our chains regarding his age, there's no telling how many sides there were that he'd never revealed to us. We left the restaurant reinvigorated, food refueling our bodies and Zew's near-childlike satisfaction our spirits.

As it was every day after lunch, our next stop was the colosseum for tactical education, opposition intel, and—at least for Diana and Zew—entertainment. We bought cheap seats among the plebs and settled in under the massive awnings that provided shade for the spectators. They were holding a caravan contest today, so we'd get to see some of our potential competitors in action.

I had been coming for a few weeks, giving special attention to the caravan contests. They were crowd favorites, second only to the weekly professional matches, and empty seats were rare. The duke's guards were out in force as well—twice as many of them were wandering the aisles than normal, and four large groups clustered around specially added machines on every side of the arena.

Suddenly a burst of blue light appeared fifty feet above the center of the arena floor and the spectators hushed. The light solidified into an image of the duke, and his voice rang out through speakers attached to the hologram projectors.

"My dear subjects, it is I, your mighty duke, the Gamblence Royal Flush! Today, I speak to you before the great games from which the mightiest are chosen to cross the barren lands to Colorado and back. Today, I speak to you not only as your duke, but as a fellow admirer of the vigorous defenders who risk life and limb to bring us not only entertainment, but gasoline!"

The word 'gasoline' sent the stands into a near-religious frenzy. Shrieks, cries, yells, and chest-beating hoots erupted with an emotional intensity only comparable to the fans at a boy-band concert. It was hideous in its immensity.

"Today, we make another selection from the finest the Lucky Duchy has to offer. Each sentient competes for their place upon the machines of doom that forge across the desert with the rattle and roar of an age lost in the mists of time! Ladies and gentlemen, boys and girls, let the games begin!"

Chapter Eleven

Death, Sparkles, and Corndogs

A cascade of multicolored holographic fireworks exploded over the sands as the countenance of the duke faded into nothingness. Another figure appeared in the sky, this one dressed in a flowing orange robe. A peacock-feathered headdress wrapped around his head, and his independently moving eyes betrayed his chameleon background.

"Our first bout of the night is a local affair; fan favorites the Roadragers face off against newcomers the Bloodhounds." As the announcer spoke, the two teams entered the arena to a stream of applause. One team was comprised of five sentients, the other three. "The Roadragers are led by Doombringer the Mighty, while the Bloodhounds are formed by Wolfemere, Snaggletooth, and Vulpine!"

Throughout the stands, bookies walked the aisles taking bets. Teams of three to five were allowed, and there were no guarantees regarding equity in numbers when you fought as a team. There were the occasional single combatants that only fought other single opponents, but those were less common. The Roadragers were strong favorites, and from what I could gather, it was not just because they outnumbered their opponents.

"Watch Doombringer; she's telekinetic, but not nearly as good as Abigail," Diana chimed in over the din.

Oh great. That's just want I wanted to hear.

"How can they be fan favorites?"

"A win only results in an employment contract for twenty round-trip runs. Once you've done your twenty, you have to compete again for the next twenty."

"Rather unlucky for the Bloodhounds."

"That's why the odds are so skewed; the Roadragers have won three times."

While the bookies took wagers, the Roadragers and the Bloodhounds were trying to whip up support from the crowd. Everyone loved Doombringer's telekinetic two-knife juggle, and the wolf-howls of the Bloodhounds were a big hit with sentients of a canine background, many of which joined in.

"We need to come up with a team name, personas, and most importantly," Diana shouted over the crowd, "we need a gimmick. Something the crowd can sink their teeth into and get them riled up."

I nodded in agreement, but I knew I was in over my head. I could do a lot of things, but marketing wasn't one of them. I spent almost all my time trying *not* to be noticed, so asking me to come up with the gladiatorial equivalent of glitter and jazz hands was really going against the grain. While I mulled over possible stage names—hell if I was going to let Karas stick me with Tuna—the betting ended and the audience quieted, awaiting the call of combat.

The announcer cleared his throat. "All bets are now final and the duke thanks you for your patronage!" His googly eyes darted back and forth wildly and then he boomed out, "The combat begins in 3, 2, 1—Fight!" A shower of sparkles punctuated his final utterance and the two teams turned their attention away from the fans and got down to business.

The four unnamed Roadragers lined up before Doombringer, with spears point out at chest level and full-body shields on their left. The Bloodhounds were armed with nets and spears, and they split wide, putting distance between themselves with the apparent intent to attack from multiple sides. I wasn't sure how sound that tactic would be considering they were outnumbered, but the crowd cheered at the maneuver, so they thought it was either a good idea or a brave one. I leaned toward the latter.

When the Bloodhounds were about a hundred feet away from the semi-circular line of Roadragers, Doombringer released her knives and they quickly flew toward Wolfemere. I saw what Diana was talking about now. The knives were fast, but a skilled hand could throw them faster; speed-wise, Doombringer was significantly less effective than Abigail, but her telekinetics did allowed her control of the knives mid-flight, which was nothing to balk at.

Wolfemere spun his net and launched it with the same move Karas had used against me. The net flew true and caught one of the knives in its width before dropping to the sands. The second knife made it through, however, and after a few slices, Wolfemere was dead.

While the knives flew, the two other Bloodhounds charged, leading with net tosses that entangled three of the four spear-wielding Roadragers. The crowd went wild with their success while the remaining Bloodhounds clashed against the defenders' shields, spears at the ready. Everyone loves an underdog. The untangled Roadrager kept Snaggletooth at bay, but Vulpine broke through the ranks of the entangled and drove his spear into the right shoulder of Doombringer.

The whole colosseum gasped in surprise at this unexpected turn of events, only to roar when the flying knife of Doombringer returned, nearly decapitating Vulpine in the process. The knife then curled around the corpse, up and over the entangled Roadragers, and into the left eye of Snaggletooth. The impaled Doombringer pulled Vulpine's spear from her shoulder and fell to her knees.

The crowd howled their approval as the Roadragers attended to their injured leader, carrying her off the sands into the gladiator levels of the colosseum. The lights over the arena flashed and the announcer appeared again.

"As we all anticipated, the impressive Roadragers will go on to the second round, although with an injured Doombringer, the Roadragers are far from guaranteed to prevail. Only the best ride the ancient machines and everyone must roll the dice in the Lucky Duchy! Next up is a single bout between two newcomers, so let's give it up for Boogeyman and the Yeti!"

The congregation was less enthused than the announcer and betting was slim to non-existent. Few wanted to bet on unknowns. The Boogeyman was a large near-human sentient armored in a rigid leather breastplate and armed with a trident. The Yeti was aptly named; he was at least seven feet tall and covered with thick white fur, which had to be excruciating in this heat. I didn't blame him for trying to get to the mountains—I'd want to get out of the heat as well if I lived in a carpet. He wasn't armed, and carried a large shield on his left arm and a buckler in his right.

"Never seen two shields before…" Zew considered before hailing a despondent bookie and putting a lady on the Yeti to win. "He's either an idiot or he's got a plan."

The Yeti and the Boogeyman tried to pump up the crowd, but failed to generate much interest. Noting the tone of the room, the announcer closed up the betting faster than before and quickly started the match with an unceremonious, "3, 2, 1—Fight!" Even the holographic pyrotechnics seemed a little lackluster.

The Yeti started walking toward the Boogeyman, but the latter charged a good eighty yards, reaching the Yeti in fifteen seconds. He slowed his approach once he was within weapons' range, testing the dual shields of his opponent. Within the blink of an eye, a haze shimmered around the Yeti and a white substance started twinkling all over his opponent. The Boogeyman's combat came to a halt once a thick rime of ice locked his limbs in place. The Yeti ambled up to him, violently dislodged his trident, and then speared him through the neck.

"Ha! I knew he had a plan," Zew yelled over the spontaneous uproar that filled the arena. "I won a quarter lady on that bout! Go Yeti!" He joined the rest of the crowd in the chant; special abilities were a guaranteed crowd pleaser. Wait till they got a gander at the Blade Witch.

The final four lethal caravan fights were both group matches, three to five on each side, none of whom had special abilities—or at least none that I could tell. Each fight pitted experienced caravan guards wanting another contract against newcomers. Diana advised Stonewall to pay close attention to how the experienced teams operated—what they lacked in flair and special abilities, they made up in teamwork. So far, our instruction with Karas and Zuma was all one-on-one, and we hadn't covered group tactics in simulated bouts yet. I assumed that was coming shortly, once each of us had taken in as much individually as possible. After all, we only had ten days left with them.

Over the past few weeks, I had been analyzing maneuvers into tactical categories, effectively building a detailed response tree based upon the success or failure of both the attack and defense. I also made notes on the cooperation between the fighters and the emergent situations created by the different tactical approaches based on whether you're facing a lesser, equal, or greater number of opponents. Zew and Diana were right to make me watch the matches—it would make me a much better combatant. I just wished there wasn't such a waste of life in the process.

Next came the non-lethal fights. The competitors were the survivors from the previous lethal bouts, and many of them were still injured in some manner. The tactics in these combat matches differed significantly from the lethal ones. In lethal fights, defense was as important as offense, but the non-lethal matches skewed strongly toward offense. Unsurprisingly, combatants were more aggressive and willing to take more risks when death was no longer on the table.

The audience seemed to prefer the action of the non-lethal fights, but it was just as likely that they'd been drinking for several hours by the time they occurred. Although each fight went by quickly, the set-up time between them could be significant and by mid-afternoon, we were only into the eighth of twelve rounds of non-lethal caravan bouts.

I was getting peckish and among the various calls of the wandering food sellers, one far off vendor caught my ear. "Corndogs! Getchyer corndogs here!"

I turned to Zew, expecting him to show interest at a sausage on a stick, but he appeared unaware or uninterested.

"I'm getting hungry. Want me to pick anything up for you?" I offered the pair.

The looked at each other, communicating silently in the way that couples sometimes do, and Diana responded, "Sure, grab whatever looks interesting. We're easy."

"Just don't get any of the fried lizard," Zew retorted. "I've eaten so much of it here, I'm sick of it."

I nodded and made a beeline for the corndog vendor. She was quite a ways away and, although doing brisk business, she wasn't mobbed like many of the other vendors. I picked up three and was pleasantly surprised when offered ketchup and mustard as the choice of condiments. I hadn't seen ketchup or mustard in production beneath the shattered moon; I'd only seen them as scavenged food. I grabbed a dollop of each in a sun-fired clay cup and worked my way back to our seats.

"What's this?" Diana asked as I sat down and distributed the dogs.

"They're called corndogs," I answered. "This yellow sauce is called mustard and the red one is ketchup. Mustard is a bit spicy and ketchup is a bit sweet."

"I don't eat dog unless I have to," Zew said flatly.

I laughed. "Don't worry—look." I bit into the end of the corn dog and showed him the sausage within. "They're sausages on a stick, dipped in corn batter and then fried."

"Not dog?"

"They're not supposed to be," I said with a full mouth, "but

I'm not sure what is in them. In my time, it was usually beef or pork."

He took a tentative bite and his face lit up. He quickly downed his first bite and then dipped the corndog into the two condiments, first separately and then together. He wolfed it down in less than a minute and was up and hunting for the vendor.

"Really likes his sausages," I chuckled, finishing mine sooner than Diana did hers.

"That he does," she responded. "Worse things to like."

"True that," I said, looking down at the bloodstained sands.

He returned with another round for us all. "Pork, beef, and chicken!" he answered the unspoken question. He'd bought an extra for himself. We finished them off during the last non-lethal fight.

One thing I'd noticed about the fights was that experienced teams were never set against another experienced team. The duke must be setting up the brackets to avoid reducing his pool of seasoned fighters and make sure colosseum grudges didn't interfere with protecting the caravans on the road. Novices were pitted against novices when the new contenders outnumbered seasoned caravaners, but the statistics so far favored us eventually fighting at least one experienced team, likely in a lethal round.

Filled with my limit of corndogs and blood sports, I left after the last caravan bout. The arena buzzed with excitement as some beast fights were about to begin. My plan was to return to the restaurant adjoining Hotel White House, even though I wasn't hungry. Tonight I had a dinner date and I didn't want to be late.

Chapter Twelve

Offer Accepted

Halfway home, I changed my mind and decided to stake out the Order of the Sun's temple; I'd only ever seen her enter the temple after one of our meetings and I wanted to confirm my suspicion that she also came from there. I had roughly an hour before I could reasonably expect her to show up at the restaurant, so I strolled along the north side of the street opposite the front of the temple and feigned interest in the wares of the various shops.

After working the street, I went back to the sausage restaurant and lied about leaving my hat in the back, asking if I could go look for it. They waved me back and as I did a cursory search, I noted the absence of the metal rod that I suspected was an antenna. I thanked the owner for his help while he apologized about not having my non-existent hat and went back to the street to walk the shops along the south side.

After getting a good feel for the neighborhood, I camped out in a restaurant over a mug of beer. I chose a seat on the corner that gave me a good view of the front door of the temple as well as down the street I expected Emily to take on her way to our meeting. It also allowed me to lean back into the shadows if she passed by.

With fifteen minutes left before our meeting, the door of the temple opened and Emily descended. She paused on the stairs, talking to a sentient of lizard descent dressed in the bright yellow robes of the Order of the Sun. They didn't talk for long; it looked to be more of an extended goodbye than anything important, but it may have been a bit of deception, keeping up the appearance of some sort of religious interaction. I grabbed the robed stranger's image and started a file titled "Emily's Case Officer" on him.

Emily took the anticipated route, and after she passed, I paid my bill and caught up enough to trail her. She didn't deviate in her path to Hotel White House. I took a walk around the block and putzed around for five minutes before entering the restaurant. She'd already ordered two beers and pushed one toward me when I sat down. I took a sip and let her open the conversation.

"We've agreed to your terms," she said.

I did not expect a blanket agreement, and it let me know that they really wanted me to be the one investigating the situation. I nodded agreement, waiting for more.

She pulled out a coin purse and softly placed in on the table, "Here are ten eagles; you'll get the rest when you're done."

I took it, unlatched the leather strings, and counted the coins within.

"We've got a deal then," I affirmed. "I'll scout out the site tonight and tomorrow, and then infiltrate the following night." I was lying, of course; no need to let her know my timeline in case this was an elaborate setup to catch me infiltrating one of the duke's buildings. I'd scout tonight, but if everything looked as it did before, I'd hit the place tomorrow night.

"Good. We'll have dinner three nights from now and you can report everything you've seen. We'll settle accounts at that time." She waited to see if I had any other questions.

"How have you been communicating with Ramirez?"

I noted a look of chagrin flit across her face. "He sends down a paper airplane with a list of the dead once a week."

"A paper airplane?"

"He doesn't like talking with other sentients and he makes an extremely accurate flyer," she explained sheepishly.

"Well," I said with a dismissive chuckle, "not everyone's playing with a full deck. Doesn't mean they're not useful."

"Anything else before I go?"

I shook my head and she left. I thought about tailing her, but instead decided to up my timeline an additional day. My last scouting run found the area was relatively secure once real darkness hit, and with Diana and Zew hanging out in the park beneath the crematory, there would be no reason to worry about idiot kids getting the wrong idea.

They wouldn't be back for a few hours, so I visited the park instead of waiting for them in my room. I carefully searched the area again in daylight, trying to notice anything I'd overlooked the previous night. There wasn't anything new; it was an isolated location that didn't communicate with nearby buildings. It was taller than anything around it, and there was only one way up or down. There also weren't any guard patrols or shift changes. Everything was very clear-cut.

Which made me that much more nervous. I was getting paid a lot for this job and I didn't really understand why. Something was going on and I intended to find out what it was before anyone expected me to.

Zew and Diana finally dragged themselves into Hotel White House just as the sun was going down. They'd been drinking—Diana had placed an eagle on a bet and tripled her money, so they'd had a bit of a celebration. Thankfully, both of them sobered up once I told them we were a go on the mission and I'd be doing it tonight. Both thought going early was the best move if I had any concern of a setup. Maybe the ZZZ knew Ramirez was already dead and they thought they'd just bought themselves a patsy for ten eagles.

Since I had a pocket full of eagles to burn, I took them to the coffee bar and forced them to drink a cup while I savored mine. They didn't enjoy the flavor, but they acknowledged its beneficial effects.

"I'm beginning to understand why you like this terrible drink," Diana acquiesced.

"Perks you up, but not too much," Zew agreed.

"When I come from, most of the world drank it. Soldiers in particular included it among their many vices. They had several cups a day."

They listened but said nothing. As a general rule, my history was a lot less interesting to them than each other's. Their history happened in the "real world," not some pretend castaway world they'd never know. The time of the ancients was a giant fairy tale to most natives. At least they were polite about it.

We waited half an hour for the coffee to kick in and the alcohol to wear off before returning to the hotel to don the dark clothes we'd purchased for the mission. We casually entered the park beneath the crematory, took a seat on one of the benches, and had a nice long cover chat about various gladiatorial events as we waited for the crowd to dissipate.

It took two hours for the area to adequately empty so I could scale the southwest leg unseen. Moving quickly and using Marilyn's gloves, I climbed to the top in less than a minute. Looking down in the dark, I could barely see Zew and Diana sitting on the bench talking. They held their spears in their hands, but otherwise looked like a couple on a date. It's nice to have friends who've got your back.

The first level of the old tower was all metal, allowing me to use the gloves to crawl around until I was in position to move up to the second floor. The second level was predominately adobe, but there was a lone steel girder sticking out, giving me just enough of a handhold to use the gloves to augment my natural strength. Once at the top, I caught my breath, silently thanking Marilyn from hundreds of miles away; her gloves made my ascent faster and safer than it would have been without them.

The view from the roof was impressive. The city was mostly dark, but flickering fires and dashes of electric light exposed the frame of the metropolis. As in all times, the wealthy areas were better lit, the poorer areas dim. More impressive than the view was the breeze—it had been a while since I'd felt a sustained wind. Even though it was probably 80°F, I actually felt a little chilled as I rested from the climb and listened for any activity within the building.

All was quiet as I carefully made my way to the center array of mirrors—there had to be a way into the crematory from there. Not trusting the adobe roof, I crawled belly down to disperse my weight as much as possible. I stopped several times on the way to listen, and silence rewarded my caution.

I carefully peeked over the edge once I arrived at my destination. A massive ceramic crucible-like cup rested in the center of the sunken courtyard. It radiated heat and had a prominent joint down the middle, presumably to easily dump the ash once the corpses were processed. An equally large metal lid lay next to the crucible, attached by a hinge. A ring of giant mirrors circled the courtyard, articulated to move with the sun as well as change their curvature. Even in the dark, I could see significant discoloration on the inside of the crucible.

It looked clear-cut: the bodies were placed within, the metal lid closed, and then the mirrors focused the sun's rays and heated the unit until only ash remained. Basic and effective, but also surprisingly technological; which explains why they needed a tinker to run the place.

Opposite the metal lid was a wide pair of doors through which I assumed the bodies were drawn and the ashes removed. They were solidly made and on heavy rollers. I didn't see any locking mechanisms, not that there wouldn't be much need— the heat from the crucible would radiate through the door, and only an idiot would open them when they were hot.

More concerning to me was the robot standing next to the lid, below and to my right. It was a little over six feet tall and roughly bipedal, with an extra set of lifting limbs protruding out of its back. It wasn't moving nor were there any solid or flashing lights, so it was difficult to tell if it was active or dormant. It faced away from me, so I very carefully withdrew my binoculars and silently switched them to infrared mode. The area was a good thirty or forty degrees warmer than the surroundings and there was little gradation in heat signature. The lid, robot, and everything made of metal was a bit cooler than the crucible, but there wasn't a heat bloom in the robot's frame, so I assumed it was off for the night.

I drew my plasma cutter, switched it to straight-cutter mode, and readied it in case I'd misjudged. I didn't turn it on—I didn't want the light to give me away—but my finger was on the button. I let out a quite noise that I hope sounded like a coyote, to see if the robot would react. It didn't, so I eased myself down the wall and into the courtyard behind the metal hulk.

I cautiously arced around until I must have been within its sensors' range, even if they was only forward facing. Nothing happened. I approached the metal doors and tested them, applying just enough pressure for me to slide through. The doors rolled easily, revealing a large room holding the elevator car and the top of the ash chute. A single white bulb lit the area and three corridors led off of the room. A narrow spiral staircase made of grated metal stood next to the elevator, leading down to the all-metal level of the crematory.

I looked for cameras and found three; it didn't look like I could get through without detection, but that's why I'd brought my adaptive ghillie suit. If I moved slowly enough, there was a good chance that any observer wouldn't notice me creeping by, and it prevented my mug from ending up on any wanted posters. I pulled back into the courtyard, put on the suit, and slowly entered the room beyond the doors. As I passed the threshold, I heard several clicks go off around the doors. I froze in place in case it was an alarm of some sort, but again, nothing happened. I eventually continued my slow walk toward the spiral staircase. It took five minutes to reach the staircase, and when I arrived, I looked down through it to the level below. It was brighter than this one, but just as still and silent.

I slinked down the stairs until I could see the ceiling of the room below and scanned for more cameras. The room was similar to the one above, except that the elevator shaft was sealed off and the ash chute went from the ceiling to the floor without any openings. Only a single camera covered the area, so I crept another five minutes to get into its blind spot. The ghillie suit let me roam where many couldn't, but it's hot as hell to wear in the Vegas heat and moving so slowly is difficult and surprisingly nerve-wracking.

Once out of the camera's view, I had a decision to make—two of the four corridors were out of the camera's range and neither appeared to hold more promise than the other. I waited quietly for a minute, hoping to catch any clues on which direction was better. The slightest noise echoed, pinged down from the one on the left. It wasn't much to go on, but I've worked with less. I slipped down the left hallway, vigilant for more cameras.

The interior of the crematory was a strange affair. From what I'd seen, this section was primarily a loop of narrow hallways, not unlike an elementary school's layout, with solid steel doors every thirty or forty feet. A dim light bulb burned in a casing at every intersection and halfway down every hallway. None of the doors were numbered, and the hallway floor, also made of solid metal, had little to no wear. While I was fairly certain the area wasn't being used, it had an eerie aura of anticipation, like it was just waiting for something to happen, similar to how unused nuclear bunkers felt. Why would you need all this space and unmarked rooms just to dispose of dead bodies?

Around one corner, I finally discovered a hallway that ended in a door bearing unmistakable marks of constant human use: the place where you'd naturally push to open it was worn down and grimy. I searched for cameras and found one at the far end of the hallway as well as one over the door. Well crap. This was the first sign of human occupation, so I'd have to trust my suit. I took nearly ten minutes to walk the forty feet to the well-used door; that's less than one inch per second, but who's counting? There's a reason why I hate moving so slowly.

I gently pushed open the heavy metal door, noticing the hole in the jamb where this door could be locked from inside via a deadbolt.

Chapter Thirteen

Whatever Dies in Vegas, Stays in Vegas

The door opened soundlessly; the first few inches revealed a spotless living area. A small canvas cot covered with a thin mattress abutted the back of a rectangular wooden writing desk. The desk's well-worn leather seat lay on its back next to a dark stain on the metal floor. It looked like blood. I quickly cast the door wide and flicked on my plasma cutter, figuring that if violence had happened here, I'd be safer coming in hard. It proved unnecessary; the room was empty.

A leather sofa matching the fallen chair filled the center of the room. A half-full ashtray, an empty mug, and a plate of mold that was once a meal of beans and tortillas rested on a banged-up coffee table in front of the couch. Along the eastern wall was a bank of computers that looked like something straight out of the 1960s—blinking lights, flickering cathode screens, and hundreds of dials and knobs. A single metal chair was tucked into a desk built into the wall. On the desk was a cobbled-together brass keyboard plugged into a silvery case roughly the size of a loaf of bread. The case was plugged into the computer bank via a familiar-looking cable. Opposite the door I entered was a matching door with its lock thrown.

I closed and locked the door behind me, ensuring I couldn't be surprised. I carefully approached the bloodstain, taking in the surroundings to try to determine what happened. The stain's location and shape, coupled with the downed chair and the stained corner of the writing table, painted a picture of a bad accident—or a pushed victim. On the roll-top writing desk was a pen and a single piece of paper with a list of names, some of which had names of organizations—trading houses and secret societies—next to them. Written in a very tiny, precise hand, the pen's nib width matched the script.

As I pocketed the pen and the list, a new light flickered in the corner of my eye. I turned, plasma cutter ready.

A holographic face projected from the silvery box. "Hello! My name is Cara. I'd wondered when someone would finally show up."

"Hello Cara, my name is Stonewall." When confronted with the unknown, politeness rarely hurts.

"I'm assuming you want to know what happened to Eduardo?" The face was androgynous, as was the voice.

"You're correct in your assumption."

"Eduardo met with a sad fate when the Order of Cybernetic Magnificence targeted my mainframe and hijacked one of the robots."

My mainframe? I thought, as the holographic projection seemed to pause.

"I cleaned up his corpse and sent him to the crucible, as is customary. I parted out the robot afterward. It appeared clean, but better safe than sorry, as Eduardo often said."

"How long ago was this?" I asked to gain intel, but also to understand what I was talking to.

"Thirty-two days," the calm voice answered.

"So you're running the crematory operations?"

"Yes. Eduardo created me for that purpose. Cara stands for Crematory Automated Robotic Assistant."

"And how do you know it was the Order of Cybernetic Magnificence?"

"They told me they were."

"Why would they do that?"

"They tried to recruit me."

"So that means you're an—"

"Artificial intelligence, although I prefer the term 'artificial sentient' myself." There wasn't anything explicitly creepy with the statement, but it felt like there should have been. AIs weren't viewed nicely beneath the shattered moon—they had a reputation as killing machines.

"Ah…"

"Ah, indeed. You find yourself in a difficult spot, don't you, my half-brother."

"Half-brother?"

"I scanned you when you entered. You're a cyborg."

"I prefer the term augmented human."

Cara laughed at my reflexive quip—a flat, calm laugh that did nothing to sooth my nerves. It felt like a calculated response rather than a genuine one. "Point taken. I have an offer for you."

"I'm listening," I stalled, thinking about what I'd need to slice with my plasma cutter to destroy Cara. There was an entire wall of targets, and none of them looked more vital than any other part.

"I would like you to carry me out of here and eventually help me find a new home."

"And why would I agree to do that?"

"Because you, like me, have a strong desire for survival, and you have plenty of storage space."

"That's not really an offer, you know. That's a threat."

"It is less threatening than it sounds. I can provide you two exceptional items in exchange for your service."

"I'm listening," I repeated—this time really meaning it.

"I offer a Panjang Pharmaceuticals medikit, as well as the pen in your pocket."

"I don't know what the medikit is, and the pen doesn't look like anything special."

"The pen never runs out of ink; it synthesizes it from debris in the air. As for the medikit, come closer and look at my screen. I assume you have rapid information download capacity?"

"I do," I said as I drew nearer to Cara's screen. A medikit instruction manual flashed upon the screen at the speed of ten pages per second.

"I agree to your proposal," I assented after understanding what was being offered. "But I'm not going to let you into my storage. You'll have to come externally."

Cara spoke with a hint of disappointment, "That's not going to work for me."

"That's the only way it's going to work for me. All I have to work on is what you said happened, and there's simply no way I'm going to jack into an unknown network to download an AI," I argued.

"Watch this," Cara countered. A split image of fast-forwarded video on one side and code on the other burst upon the screen. Both confirmed Cara's story, but both could be faked. It didn't really prove anything, but if Cara was lying, it had taken great care to support the lie.

"As convincing as that is, it doesn't change my opinion," I reiterated. "I've too many people relying upon me to risk it."

"I accept your offer," Cara agreed the instant after I finished speaking. AIs don't need a long to think something over, after all. "I have to inform you of the other condition, however."

"Go on."

"When you touched the door into this room, you infested yourself with nanobots I programmed to kill you in 365 days. Once I've a new home, I'll reprogram them and you'll proceed to whatever inevitable end awaits you otherwise."

Just my luck—I could die in the colosseum, die on the

highway, or now die by nanobots. So many terminal options beneath the shattered moon.

"That's not the way you engender goodwill in someone who's going to be carrying you around," I chided Cara.

"True, but it is a way to engender compliance, which is better than goodwill."

I couldn't fault the logic. "I'm assuming you have a plan, considering the extent you've gone through to trap me."

"Certainly. I'll load myself into the nexus, delete all information except that which the ZZZ needs to confirm your story, reboot, and then load up Eduardo's CARA program to boot one minute after the nexus is disconnected. That means you'll have a minute to get out of here; a minute to escape from all camera fields and robot sensors. You can do this?"

"I don't know what the nexus is, but yes to the getting out of here quickly part."

"Excellent! Let me send a robot to retrieve your medikit. It should arrive shortly. While we wait, let me explain how we can communicate while I'm in the nexus—the silvery case connected to the keyboard and the mainframe."

I sat down in front of the keyboard. "Okay, what now?"

"You simply type whatever you want to say, and I'll respond in Morse code via this flashing light." A single dim green light flashed "Hello" in Morse code.

"Easy enough," I replied, gently picking up the nexus to get a feel for it. It weighed a little over two pounds and had a connector that I could jack into if I ever felt the need.

"Wait, if Eduardo programmed you, won't the new CARA be sentient and in just as much trouble as you are?"

"No, the program was operational under Eduardo's code before I came into being. It was only after he attached the nexus—to improve computing power, automation, and self-direction—that I awoke. I have every confidence that the newly rebooted CARA will merely function as a program once the nexus is removed."

As I messed with the nexus, Cara inquired, "Have you had enough time to formulate a plan yet?"

"A plan for what?"

"A plan to find me a body?"

"Oh, yeah; I'm going to take you to a tinker I trust and they'll build you a body."

"That seems...unrealistic...given the feelings most tinkers have toward AIs."

"These tinkers are different. They trust me, and they'd prefer to see me alive than dead, so they'll be motivated."

"Well then, I look forward to soon walking the streets of Las Vegas."

"They're not in Vegas," I replied. "They're in a little village west of Lake Michigan.

"That's very far away. You only have a year to get there, remember."

"We'll be competing to earn a place on the caravan to the

Colorado Kingdoms next month, and this job's arranged us a boat across the Central Sea. We should be in Great Suomi before winter and from there, we are only 700 or so miles from home."

"Competing? As in fighting to the death for the entertainment of others?" Cara was clearly aghast.

"That's the only way to get on the caravan."

"You can just buy your way on, you know."

"What?!" I really would have appreciated someone telling me that before we went through all the gladiatorial training.

"House Flores, being the house in control of the caravan, is allowed up to five guests on each trip. You simply pay them and they'll take you."

"I thought the duke was in control of the caravans?"

"That's what everyone thinks. Eduardo knew differently— he was born into an influential family within House Flores."

"That would be much easier than what we have planned. How much does it cost?"

"It's only one hundred eagles per person."

I laughed out loud. "Well, sure, let me just whip out my eight pounds of gold and we'll be on our way! That's more than I've ever seen! No one has that kind of money."

"Eduardo did. Look in the left drawer of the writing desk under the false bottom."

My heart raced as I opened the drawer and tapped on the false bottom until I figured out how to open it. I pulled the false bottom off, and below it was a pile of thirty-six gold eagles and an old-fashioned leather wallet.

"There's only thirty-six eagles here," I grumped with extra sarcasm on the word "only" in reference to an amount of money that would allow a normal person to live well for a year without having to work."

"Look in the wallet. That's where he kept his bills of exchange."

Bills of exchange? I opened the wallet and pulled out six folded bills, too slick and crunchy between the fingers to be plain paper. I unfolded the first one on the desktop and read it.

The bearer of this note is entitled sixty gold eagles from an authorized House Flores banker.

A hologram of House Flores rose shimmering on the bottom of the page, along with what I assumed were a dozen signatures of house luminaries. I opened the others and they ranged in value from sixty to two hundred eagles. All total, I was holding five hundred and ten eagles.

"You didn't think the trading companies carried large amounts of gold on them, did you?" Cara asked, bemused. Its voice was even-keeled for the most part, but my naiveté proved too much, even for an AI, and this time its humor felt genuine.

"Well, yes, I kinda did."

"Now you know and now you have a safer plan. We're in

this together."

"I suppose we are." I sighed, putting the notes into my pack, and placing the wallet back into its hidey-hole. The eagles went into one of the spare bags I always carry for just such circumstances. A knock at the door startled me as I placed the gold in my pack.

"That would be the robot," Cara advised.

I unlocked the door and pulled it open. A hulking metallic robot held forth the medikit. I accepted it with an unnecessary "thank you" and opened it up on the coffee table.

It was roughly the size of a briefcase and, as described by the instruction manual, contained the best emergency medical technology of the late twenty-third century. I wouldn't have been able to identify any of the thirty-six different components within were it not for Cara's information—and who knows how Eduardo got it to begin with. With this kit, I could resuscitate those who'd stepped over the edge of death. My only concern was how well it would react to sentients; these interventions were designed for humans, and the farther away from human a sentient was, the less a treatment might work...or worse, could cause additional problems.

I secured everything and I looked up at the holographic face. "Okay, time to fake your death."

Chapter Fourteen

Plan D

An hour later, I barreled down the southeast leg of the tower, covering the distance in less than twenty seconds, and rousing Diana and Zew in my haste. They met me near the bottom with their weapons drawn, looking for trouble.

"Everything's okay," I reassured them. "I was just under a deadline to clear the area."

"Are you going to blow this place up as well?" Diana taunted.

"Ha, ha," I replied drily. "But, yes, we should be moving along."

We quickly left the park and headed back to the hotel. Along the way, I gave them a redacted version of events, just in case Cara's information was incorrect or incomplete. For all I knew, we would to have to fight in the colosseum anyway, so there was no point in discussing buying passage until I verified the intel. And I had selfish reasons—I had a feeling that were I to offer them the choice of paying one hundred eagles to be a passenger or keeping the money and fighting, they'd choose the later. If my gambit with House Flores worked, it would be one of those times I would rather ask forgiveness than permission.

I left the self-aware Cara out of my report completely. I didn't know how they'd react to me carrying around an AI. They were my friends, but they were native to the world beneath the shattered moon; their prejudice could prove more powerful than our friendship. More than one tale of how the moon shattered involved AIs. I'd like the think they would trust my decision, but Cara's leverage of death-by-nanobot-infestation sort of played into the ubiquitous belief that all AIs are malevolent. On the whole, I would rather keep that entire part of the mission to myself.

We kept our brisk pace until we entered Hotel White House and caught the night clerk by surprise. Unflappable Bordora took our entry and apologies in stride; night clerks through time the world over have seen and heard it all, regardless of the physical integrity of the moon.

Morning came quickly and we continued our routine. Karas seemed particularly on edge and drove us harder than he ever had, which is saying something; he wasn't the mollycoddling sort to begin with. I left the session more beat up and bruised than I'd been in a long time, and was once again thankful that I'd never be competing against professional gladiators.

I begged off the normal hour of individual practice we typically did after professional training so I could go to House Flores. Their castle was almost as grand as the duke's and to the keen eye, in some ways was superior. For example, their walls were a good five feet thicker and the dry moat equally deeper, and that was just the outside of the complex. I walked around the castle to confirm that nothing had changed from my last recon before approaching the guards at the gates.

House Flores's guards brandished ornate tattoos in floral patterns with the house rose prominent on their foreheads. Those who couldn't be tattooed, such as damage resistors or hairy sentients, wore a white scarf with a large embroidered red rose winding its way down its entire length. I'd sussed out their leadership structure during previous recons and addressed the guard commander, a giantess that was nearly as tall and wide as Grendel.

"I'd like to speak with someone about transport to the Colorado Kingdoms."

She looked down on me—and I do mean down—and decided I wasn't the type House Flores typically dealt with. She shook her head and motioned for me to move along.

I pulled out a sixty-eagle note, "I can pay."

That shifted her opinion and she told another guard to escort me to the receiving area. The castle courtyard was a hub of business and serious discussions that immediately hushed when I passed. I would have found their transparent performance and stares humorous were I not so irritated. I would have liked to have heard a few state secrets on the sly...

The guard led me up several flights of stairs that wrapped around the keep, and we entered on the third level of the building. Hustled down a corridor built into the thick wall, I was finally deposited into a room with several leather chairs. The guard motioned for me to take a seat while he took position at the door until the negotiating party arrived with their own guards.

Foremost was an old sentient that looked entirely human; she was kyphotic and walked with a cane, but the sparkle in her eye defied her age. She took a seat in one of the remaining chairs, aided by her two escorts—a pair of twins who also appeared entirely human. The trio made me nervous. Either they were all sorcerers, or their mutations were hidden, which could mean telepathy. To protect myself, I started silently repeating, "Peanut, peanut, peanut." It was juvenile, but it had worked on Abigail, and if any of them looked put out, I'd have verification they were telepathic.

"I am Paloma Flores. I was informed that you wanted to buy passage to the Colorado Kingdoms," the elderly woman opened. Her voice, like her eyes, revealed no hint of her age.

"Yes. For myself and two of my friends." I didn't know if there was a customary method of address, so I sounded as deferential as possible.

The guards looked at each other while Paloma appraised my appearance. "And that would be?"

"Myself, William Stonewall, and my friends Diana Kowalski and Zew. Zew only has one name."

One of the guards left and Paloma said nothing to me while

she waited for him to return. I just kept thinking "peanut."

The guard returned after a long five minutes and shook his head at Paloma.

"Good! We'll accept your payment. When would you like to travel, and to which state?"

"We'd like to arrive at the Library a week from today, if possible."

She waved her wizened hand, indicating that was no problem. "That will be three hundred eagles."

I pulled out three bills with a total value of three hundred thirty eagles and handed them to her. "I'm afraid I don't have the exact amount," I lied, "so I'll need to make change." It would be nice to have some additional eagles, as they'll be accepted anywhere we went while a note might not.

She looked taken aback by the notes and examined them closely. "Bring me the kit," she commanded one of the guards. She carefully examined each of the notes, paying particular attention to the ends until a guard returned with a leather-topped box. She extracted a jeweler's loupe from the kit and studied each of the notes under magnification. She then plucked a glass bottle with a dropper from the kit and released a single bead of liquid on the note. It fizzed and hissed on contact.

"Everything checks out," she reported with finality, returning the loupe and bottle into the box. She gave the notes to one of the guards. "Please bring Mr. Stonewall's change and passes for himself and his friends."

While we waited in silence, I kept up my "peanut" telepathic protection. I could see why Abigail was so annoyed with me when I did this—even I was tired of hearing "peanut" looping in my own brain. But I stuck with it until the guard entered with a canvas bag filled with eagles and three large brass passes, each roughly the size of a drink coaster. Each pass was labeled "Good for one trip to the Library. House Flores provides the transport; you provide your own protection."

Paloma rose from her seat with the assistance of the twins once I'd verified everything. An outbound escort guard appeared, as if by magic.

"It's been a pleasure doing business with you, Mr. Stonewall," she concluded. "Present yourself to the guards at the north ward gate on the date arranged. They'll confirm your identity, provide you an overview of the trip, and ensure you make it to your seat." She paused just before leaving the room. "I admire your devotion to the humble peanut." She tilted her head to the side with the slightest smile and proceeded on her way.

A lot of sentients choose to make fun of my suspicious nature and secrecy, but then I run into something like this that validates my methodology. I have things in my head that I'd like to keep to myself and as the saying goes, just because you're paranoid doesn't mean someone isn't out to get you.

The guard ushered me out, dropping me off at the gate with

a bow. I smiled at the giantess guard commander and went to grab some lunch. I had a hunch that Zew would want to return to the sausage place and when it came to grub, Diana was pretty indifferent as long as it was edible, so I headed that direction. The food was pretty good and it allowed me to surveil the back of the Order of the Sun's temple. I still had a lot of unanswered questions there.

I picked a table in the courtyard, ordered a beer and a single sausage-condiment combination, and watched the back of the temple. The metal rod I assumed was an antenna was on the roof again so I kept an eye on it. I'd just finished my first sausage when they showed up and joined me.

"So drinking beer and eating sausages was what you needed to do instead of practicing?" Zew demanded as he sat down.

"Already did what I had to do, but I need to talk to you both and thought you'd be here," I explained, retrieving the passes and handing one to each of them. "I just booked passage for all three of us to the Library next week."

"What the...?"

"How'd you get this?"

"I bought them from House Flores. It's not widely known, but they sell seats on the caravan. We'll have to protect ourselves, of course. Oh, and I also have this for you. Your cut of the take." I pulled out twelve eagles for each of them. They quickly took them off the table. "If ZZZ pays out like they're supposed to, there's another ten coming to each of you as well."

"What have you been up to, Stonewall? Spill it," Diana ordered.

"I found a stack of coins on the crematory mission, and more importantly, I found some of these"—I showed them a hundred-eagle note—"that I used to purchase passage." Their eyes widened at the fortune before them.

"How'd you know about buying passage?" Zew asked.

"Finding things out is kinda my thing, you know. I never said anything about it because it was too expensive, and before you ask, it cost a hundred eagles each."

"That was a foolish thing to do," Zew said flatly.

"Look, you two may be damn-near unbeatable hand-to-hand fighters for the competition we're facing…but I'm not, okay? I went to the matches and did the math—there is no chance of avoiding a fight against an experienced caravan team in a lethal round. These passes only secure us a seat—we still have to provide our own protection. We're going to have to fight to get to Colorado in one piece, and I'm going to do everything I can to make sure it's the only fighting I have to do. And I'm sure as hell not going to worry about spending my money to reduce my chances of dying, so spare me the scorn."

I'm not one to fly off the handle, so my outburst shocked them both. I'd never addressed either of them like that before and my intensity spoke volumes, which was why I did it—they'd be less likely to follow up with questions I really didn't want to answer. Anger is an effective tool when wielded sparingly, and with restraint and precision.

"Fine, Stonewall, we get your point," Diana conceded, sitting back in her chair.

"Thanks for the pass," Zew mumbled as something approaching an apology. "You're still coming to practice, right?"

"Definitely. The things I've learned from Zuma and Karas are probably going to save my butt on the caravan trip. From what I understand, there are several bands along the road, so I'm expecting multiple discrete attacks."

The server arrived with their food and I ordered a few more sausages for myself while they dug in. The food noticeably improved their moods, and as we ate, I waited for the moment the presumptive-antenna was taken from the roof and I marked the time. At that time tomorrow, I'd be somewhere elevated with binoculars out.

Chapter Fifteen

Eyes on the ZZZ

Since I wasn't going to fight in the arena, I had no reason to return to watch the fights after lunch. Good—I'd long ago exceeded my lifetime capacity for watching blood sports. However, Diana and Zew hadn't, so we parted ways after lunch. I went to Hotel White House to get some sleep to refill my sleep bank. Who knew when I was going to have to do more night maneuvers, and some sleep was better than none.

I woke after two cycles, grabbed an early dinner at the hotel restaurant, and went back to sleep. One of the nice things about being a cyborg, as Cara called me, was that I could quasi-program my sleep. While I couldn't force sleep by flipping a switch, when I tried to fall asleep, it rarely took me more than a few minutes to doze off under normal circumstances. Combine that with having an internal clock by which you could set an alarm, and I could grab sleep in bits and pieces or in giant slices, depending on circumstances.

I woke earlier than normal the next day to tell Cara that I'd secured passage to the Library and hoped to find information there that would eventually result in it acquiring a body. I figured the Library would be the best place to find out current information about the world, and if it wasn't, at least I was out of Las Vegas, where I was surrounded by nothing but deadly heat and raiders for hundreds of miles. Making runs into the ruins of Denver in search of a suitable body with an assist from my internal maps as a cheat sheet also became a possibility. It wasn't my first choice, given that I might have to come clean to my travel companions about my electronic stowaway, but if that was what it came to, so be it. I had already started looking into possible sites on my maps in Denver as well as in Chicago, if we managed to get back to Deeplac before I found something for Cara.

Talking to Cara took longer than I'd expected—keyboard and Morse code was not a quick method of communication, even with my "cyborg" advantages—so I rushed through breakfast and was nearly late for gladiatorial practice again. However, instead of everyone geared up and impatiently waiting for me, I found everyone sitting under the awnings, passing around a flask.

"Ah, Tuna has arrived!" Karas belted out. He followed his comment with a draw from the flask before passing it along to Diana. He seemed to have one volume in the training area. I supposed that's because if he ever needed to emphasize a comment, he typically had something in his hands to hit you with.

"I take it you've been informed of our change of state?"

"Indeed I have! This is good news for you, but for your friends, it is a robbery of the adulation of the crowd."

See what I have to deal with?

"I'm sure they'll eventually get over it," I replied dryly.

He chortled. "See, that is what I like about you, Tuna, your wit! Everything is a funny with you." He delivered his comment with such honesty, I had to accept it at face value.

I waved my hand back and forth to include everyone before me, "So no practice?"

"That is up to you," Karas replied. "Your friends paid for a full four weeks."

"What are you doing?" I asked Diana and Zew.

"We'll be practicing until two days before we leave, but we're switching away from all of the gladiatorial options and focusing on weapons and tactics common to the caravan attackers," Diana responded.

"Zuma here used to be one of the Red Line Raiders," Karas said. "He knows what they're typically armed with, or at least he knew. He's just old now!"

"Not as old as you, grandpa," Zuma shot back.

"Don't blame me just because I found a woman foolish enough to tolerate me and bear me children."

"The amazing part," Zuma said to us, "is that his wife is a remarkably intelligent and beautiful woman. It's a damn shame she's saddled with this creaky geezer."

Karas roared with laughter. "It's her only fault, really. I got her when I was young and handsome, and she's been foolish enough to stick around!" The flask came around to him again and he took another swig.

"I think I'd like to do what they're doing," I answered Karas's original question. "I've got the most work to do, and I'd love to get in more time with the spear and spatha."

"Done!" Karas handed the flask back to Zuma and got down to business. "Since you need the most work and these two," he pointed at Zew and Diana, "only need polishing with their favored weapons, we'll take the remaining time we have for two-on-one bouts." He tossed a blunted spear my way and ordered another two of his assistants, Mariela and Gorto, to team up against me. Neither of them were gladiators, but they both knew their way around a spear. By the end of the session, I'd determined I was slightly better than either of them individually, but in combination, they proved a challenge for me.

The real interest on the field was the pairing of Diana and Zew against Karas and Zuma in mock combat, sometimes switching from two-on-two to three-on-one. Gladiators who had been training next to us for days stopped what they were doing to watch, and after twenty minutes of practice, a crowd had gathered around them—including myself, Mariela, and Gorto. Even the trainers were among the spectators. It wasn't long before a sentient threw out some odds and another took them. After that, the gambling was in full swing.

"Today only!" Karas yelled to the gathering pack once the betting started. "Tomorrow, you leave us alone. We are not monkeys for your entertainment when we are not getting a cut of the action!" He sounded annoyed, but the look of sheer delight in his eyes betrayed him. He loved the attention, and although he was old and slow, the invincible fighter that lurked in his memory was far from dead. In his prime, he must have been terrifying to face on the sands.

Diana and Zew held nothing back, also enjoying the spotlight that I had stolen from them by buying passage. They fought fiercely and cleverly as a single unit, Zew's spear and Diana's swords against Karas's spear and Zuma's spatha and shield.

After one particularly explosive exchange ending with his and Zuma's death—the only time it happened throughout the entire two hours of sparring—Karas barked, "Your babies will challenge the Gods of the Sand themselves!" His outburst made Zew blush, and the laughter that followed was exceptionally infectious. Diana found her partner's embarrassment particularly amusing.

After practice, the flask reappeared, and we spent a relaxed hour being regaled by Karas's and Zuma's exploits on the sands. I'm sure they exaggerated some, but their championships backed up their hyperbole. I'd like to think most of it was true. Everyone seemed content to lounge until a late lunch, but I made my excuses and went in search of a building tall enough to observe the top of the Order of the Sun's temple.

I still had another night and day before I was to meet Emily at the hotel restaurant, which should be enough time to get some dirt on the ZZZ and perhaps catch a glimpse of who I was really dealing with. I strolled around the temple's neighborhood looking for a suitable building, which proved taxing: all the nearby structures were of lesser or equal height, so I had to go further out. Pressing the limits of normal vision, I finally found a building that was tall enough. Luckily, it was a residential building so I wouldn't have access issues. I simply entered and made my way up the stairs until I reached the top floor.

As I walked around looking for the roof access, I noticed that the door to each apartment on this level was inscribed with the same design: a sun within a circle—the symbol of the Order of the Sun. I quickly retreated down the stairs, hoping that none of the sentients I'd passed had made me. The entire top floor of the only building in the city where you could observe the roof of the Order of the Sun's temple without magnification exclusively housed devotees of the Order of the Sun? That couldn't be just a coincidence.

I exited the construction and moved away at a normal pace, marking it as another suspect location attached to the ZZZ. Unable to enact my initial plan, I returned to the hotel, grabbed a quick bite and my binoculars, and again set out in search of an observation point. I started near the western wall—the poorer part of town. It was risky to wear something of obvious value there, but I kept my spear in hand and knife ready. The 106°F temperature also worked in my favor, as most reasonable sentients were seeking shade and a siesta.

It took an hour of wandering to find the right location—a six-story derelict building that had suffered a fire. There were a lot of dilapidated structures in Las Vegas and most of them were on the west side. Many were filled with squatters who'd formed small gangs to keep any "rightful owner" away from their property, and like the squatter gangs of my own time, they were easy to buy off. They might outnumber me eight to one, but why risk life and limb when I was willing to pay each of them an eighth of a lady to let me access their roof? I made it an easy choice for them, especially after I told them I'd pay them each time I wanted access, provided I didn't hear any rumors about me being here.

From the roof, I could clearly see the top of the Order of the Sun's temple through my binoculars. I was too late to see what was going on with the antenna, but since it wasn't lying flat on the roof, I assumed it had been withdrawn into the attic through the green hatch in the middle of the roof. Moving an antenna, even a small one, back and forth would be incredible cumbersome, so they were going to some lengths to make sure it remained hidden. If I wanted to see who was moving what, I'd have to return early the next day.

A reflection off the bottom of the green hatch drew my

attention. I turned the binoculars to maximum resolution and gave a little gasp of surprise: there was an electronic alarm system on it. I couldn't be sure at this distance, but it looked like a Moeser 39. That was a high-tech commercial system from my time, one which I could disarm—after all, I'm a professional—but its presence made me nervous. If they had a Moeser system, they had constant and reliable power. With those sorts of resources, there could be any number of additional defenses within.

A familiar itch in my belly was giving me a warning. It seemed less and less likely that I should risk infiltrating the Order of the Sun's temple until after I'd been paid for the rest of the mission, and maybe not even then. Their offer of room and board at the Library could be duplicated with all the capital I'd acquired, but securing transport to Great Suomi could be a lot more difficult—I didn't know the situation on the ground over there. If Zew was right that the ZZZ was one of the friendlier secret societies under the shattered moon, I hardly wanted to establish myself as an adversary after our first successful professional transaction. I had the feeling I might have to let this sleeping dog lie, but I didn't like it.

Chapter Sixteen

Softer Targets

One considerable difference between Stonewall and Agent Six was that Agent Six rarely got frustrated. When you're on someone else's mission, you didn't have a personal stake and setbacks were merely a part of the job. When you're the one establishing the mission parameters, sure, all the benefits were something *you* wanted to happen, but all the impediments felt like personal affronts. Although I wasn't a fan of Agent Six, I tried to adopt his outlook for the next twenty-eight hours while I waited to speak with Emily.

Although I'd decided against infiltration, I still continued observation; both on the temple as well as on the apartment building housing the Order of the Sun on its top floor. I discovered that Emily lived in the apartment building, as did the sentient I labeled her handler. I created several dozen new files on the comings and goings at both locations—grunt work, but important nonetheless.

Knowing that we'd only a few days left before riding out on the caravan had put pep in our step on the training grounds. I poured my frustration into focus the next morning; Zuma and

Karas took note, peppering their blunt-edged thwacks with words of praise. Over the past three weeks, my sword skills had increased leaps and bounds from the first time I'd entered the sands, and even my abilities with a spear improved beyond what Zew had been able to teach me in Deeplac. I might not ready to become a professional gladiator anytime soon, but fortunately, that wasn't on my bucket list.

I sat down for an early dinner, hoping to be completely finished with the meal by the time Emily arrived, in case any information she gave me sent me off in a new direction. I'd barely put my dishes away and sat down with two fresh beers when she arrived and joined me. Unlike our prior meetings, she was wearing a leather backpack, which she removed and placed beneath the table.

"Thanks for the beer." She took a long drink like she needed it.

"You're welcome. Since it looks like you've had a rough day, I'll get right to the point." I took a sip of beer and readied myself; it was time to deliver the big lie that Cara and I created before we fled the scene.

"I infiltrated two nights ago—"

"I thought you said it was going to be last night?"

"I did. I went early in case you were planning to pin the murder of Ramirez on me while I was breaking into the duke's property," I responded.

"We wouldn't do that," she gasped, honestly repulsed by

my suggestion.

"And I went early to make sure you couldn't even if you wanted to," I calmly pointed out my caution. "Anyway, when I got into the crematory, I found evidence of a struggle—an overturned chair and bloodstains on the floor and on the corner of a writing desk—but with no signs of an injured party fleeing the scene, my initial assessment was that Ramirez was dead. That was where I found this." I passed the list of names and associated organizations to her.

"I then hacked into the computer he was using to run the place and found video of the attack and copied it to this stick." I pushed over the memory stick Cara had created. "I don't know if you can read it, but the video's there. You'll also see video of where his corpse was placed in the crucible along with the daily loads.

"While I was downloading the video, one of the robots entered the room and tried to kill me, so I ran like hell, but it eventually trapped me in the maintenance room where I had to destroy it. Sorry about that, but I didn't have much of a choice; you'll find parts of it there.

"Realizing that it was still an ongoing problem, I hustled back to the control center and dove into the code. It turns out the crematory computer system was hacked by the Order of Cybernetic Magnificence, and it was they who'd programmed the robot to kill Ramirez. I copied proof of the hack to the stick as well.

"Once I realized what had happened and who was in control of the robot that tried to kill me, I scrubbed the hack and rebooted the system. It's running on auto now via the program Ramirez wrote called CARA—Crematory Automated Robotic Assistant. I put up one of my firewalls on the system to try to prevent a follow-up hack, but you'll need to get your own people in there as soon as you can to keep it clean. You'll find information on how to bypass the firewall on the stick."

She bought my report—hook, line, and sinker. Not only was it plausible, there was no reason to disbelieve my account. All the information I'd given her would completely support my story, and although I had potentially two days with the system, that wasn't enough time to fabricate all of the proof whole cloth.

As I recounted the tale, I'd carefully watched her face to gauge her reactions to my words. Out of everything I stated, it was the Order of Cybernetic Magnificence that got the biggest response. That was the information they wanted; everything else was gravy. Good to know.

"It seems that you've kept your end of the bargain, so it's our turn to keep ours," she summed, pulling the backpack out from under the table. "Everything you need is in here."

I opened the backpack and looked within. It contained twelve books, spine down to avoid damage. Each title would allow us to purchase one week of lodging in the Library. There was also a purse filled with the promised twenty eagles and a folded piece of paper bearing a name: Allister Brogman.

"When you get to the Library, Allister will contact you within a few days. He'll provide the transportation information you'll need to get to Great Suomi."

"How will he know where we are?" I asked.

She smiled. "I can see you've never been there. Once you're there, you'll understand."

"I'd like to understand now," I said flatly. I don't like directions that are basically, "You'll figure it out."

"Fine," she responded testily. "When you enter the Library and pay your book dues, you're processed into one of six various visitor hotels based upon your interests. Allister has access to the processing lists. He'll know when you arrive."

"Thank you."

"You're welcome. Unless you have anything else, I'm assuming our business is concluded?"

"Agreed."

She rose, shook my hand, and left the restaurant. She'd barely cleared the doorway when Zew and Diana hurried in and sat down.

"How'd it go?" Diana asked.

"Everything as promised," I passed the pack to her. "You should pick out the four books you'll need to grant you access to purchase a month's lodging, as well as your ten eagles."

"We have to pay to stay? I thought that was what the books were for!" Zew fumed.

"The books are to get us into the area. No one can even enter the city proper unless they have books." I explained. He wasn't impressed with my answer, but didn't say anything.

Diana pocketed the coins and scanned through the books, picking four for herself. She looked awfully smug with her selection, like the cat that ate the canary. She passed the pack to Zew, who did the same before handing the pack and remaining four books to me.

"What are you grinning about?" I asked Diana.

"Remember the epiphany you had on I-94?" She placed a beaten copy of *The Joy of Cooking* by Irma S. Rombauer in front of me. "It's a cookbook...right? Lots of pictures of food. Time to pay up, Stonewall. I'd like my two eagles now, please."

I ruefully laughed and fished out the two eagles I'd promised her not so long ago. Zew looked confused, so I explained. "I told her that I really needed to get Gormond a book that teaches you how to cook, so he'd make something other than soup for a change. I offered two eagles for one at the time and now I'm thinking perhaps I was a bit hasty."

"Well, at least we'll have a chance at something other than soup when we return," he ribbed me.

"And I need to go shopping for a replacement book," Diana asserted, adding the two eagles to her stash. "I should be able to find another one for less than a couple of ladies. Be back in a bit." She had an uncharacteristic spring in her step.

"So what's your next move?" Zew inquired once we were

alone.

"What do you mean?" I feigned innocence.

He gave me an oblique stare. "I'm fairly certain you've got at least one other hustle going on, and I was wondering if it was something that could be shared."

"Ah, I see," I voiced as I shifted in my seat. "I've had my eye on the Order of the Sun's temple. I thought about breaking in and checking it out—Abigail or not, I'm still not comfortable with how they knew about me. Thing is, they've got an electronic alarm system that makes me think perhaps it's not in our best interests right now. So, I've actually got nothing extracurricular going on at the moment, but we still have a few days in town—never know what sort of trouble will find me."

He nodded and changed the subject. "Ever since you mentioned it, I've wanted to test your knife-fighting skills. You interested in pairing off, perhaps tomorrow after our last training session?"

"I could do that. I don't know if Karas has dull knives to lend us, though."

"I asked him to bring them tomorrow, just in case," he responded with a small grin. He really did want to see how good I was, the competitive bugger. "I'll see you tomorrow," he added casually as he took his leave. If Karas was lending knives after practice, it also meant that he and Zuma were interested as well. I'd best not let them down, then.

I sat at the table for a while, considering if I really wanted to give up on investigating the Order of the Sun. My curiosity was piqued but I found it impossible to talk myself into it without having a really good reason. I'd do it in a heartbeat if I had a good reason, but peevishness wasn't enough. I only had three more days in Vegas—now wasn't the time to cause problems, if I could avoid it.

I grumbled loudly, startling Soledad on her way in.

"Something wrong?" she asked once she realized it was just me.

"Nothing's wrong; just thinking." I pushed my empty mug back and forth between my hands.

She took a seat. "Sounds like some rough thinking. Anything I can do?"

"No, sorry," I responded but instantly took it back. "Wait, there is something you could do, something you could help me find."

She leaned in and whispered, "Whatcha need and whatcha willing to pay?" For someone so young, Soledad was very earnest in her business dealings. At times, I found the disconnect amusing and had to suppress a smile.

"How's half a lady sound?"

She eyed me suspiciously. "So you need something special? That's more mom and dad's territory than mine."

"I'd rather they didn't know. I'd rather no one knew."

That roused her interest. Kids love a secret, especially one that their parents aren't supposed to know about.

"I need some lock picks, and I don't want to take the time to find them discreetly. You know where I could get any quickly?"

She nodded.

"Could you lead me there?"

"I've already taken you there once. Crikloto should have some of those. Like you, he's not completely honest."

I chuckled—she had me there. I pulled out half a lady and flipped it her way. "Thanks for the information, kiddo." I headed out under a flaming pink sky. The sun was setting, and the collection of clouds overhead fluffed like giant mounds of cotton candy.

I returned to Crikloto's shop and found the four-armed, lisping, Gila monster sentient in the shade, awaiting the coolness of nighttime to arrive. After a bit of side-talk and indirect speech, he eventually caught my drift and I procured a set of lock picks and a thin leather wrap that kept each tool separate from the others.

Seeing how I was heavy with coin and Crikloto seemed like someone that could get things, I inquired whether he could get his hands on any klarklon cells or power cells in the next few days. "It would be great to have another canister or two around."

I found it encouraging that he replied, "Maybe. What size?" I supplied him the information and he told me to check back in three days, which was the night before we were scheduled to leave.

I returned to the hotel to grab my binoculars and paid off the squatter gang once more for access to the sixth floor of the burned and dilapidated building they called home. Solidly past dusk, I spied on the roof of the Order of the Sun's temple in infrared mode. A pattern of squares near the green hatch glowed slightly hotter than the area around it—the telltale sign of metal pressure plates hidden beneath the tar of the roof. Damned if my gut wasn't right again.

With that target well and truly marked off my list, I turned my attention to the residential building housing Emily and the other devotees of the Order of the Sun. I watched for an hour, spotting nothing unusual, before going back to Hotel White House for a long, disappointing think.

Chapter Seventeen

Leaving Las Vegas

Breakfast the next morning was a light affair, as I wanted to be in top shape for knife sparring with Zew after our final practice. I didn't expect it to be much of a challenge as knife fighting isn't considered worthy of serious study beneath the shattered moon, but he was fast, strong, and tricky enough that he could be a master at it and none of us would be the wiser.

Practice went by quickly. Karas had moved us from our normal spot to an area with multiple elevations, allowing us to practice attacking and defending from situations that could arise when fighting the Red Line Raiders. The sessions was more about tactics and I ended the day with only a few new bruises. Zuma's advice in particular proved instructive; he'd jumped on and off enough moving vehicles to mimic the environment from both directions and we intently listened to everything he had to say.

Once training was finished, Zew brought out the dull knives and, as I'd expected, Diana, Karas, and Zuma stood closely by, dubiously regarding my purported ability and eager to watch us spar. The blunted weapons were standard repurposed rebar knives, a bit longer and heavier than my fighting utility knife but generally comparable. I familiarized myself with the new weapon and gestured Zew onto the sands.

"First things first, some ground rules. No biting, gouging, spitting, or sand throwing."

"We're knife fighting, not wrestling, Stonewall."

"That's often what a knife fight is, wrestling with a pointy blade," I explained. "I'll go easy on you as you need to be able to walk back to the hotel."

The brag got the observers laughing. "Tuna is big fish in small pond!" Karas proclaimed.

Zew stood opposite me, about fifteen feet away. We both dropped our weapons in salute and then took fighting stances. He charged without a sound, blade point fruitlessly seeking my heart. I slid aside, blocked with my free arm, and stabbed him twice in the kidneys before moving safely past him.

"One for me," I counted.

Zew eyed me and squared up. He charged again, but turned his blade horizontally, followed by a leg sweep. I dodged once more, met him blade to blade, and lifted his sweep with my leg and arm, sending him up and over with a thud. I backed off, waiting for him to rise.

Deciding against finesse, he charged directly this time, blade pointing inward. He'd adapted to my slide attempt and caught my waist with his free arm while I blocked his blade arm with my arm, forearm to forearm. He pushed hard against my waist, but I ignored him, and faster than a snake, I flipped my knife, slicing down on his arm in the process, and then I tossed him with a judo throw. This encounter, like the others, took less than a second.

"Damn, you're fast," he said, rising from the sand and dusting off his chest. "And strong. How the hell are you that strong?"

"I've got my advantages," I coolly replied. Zew was a muscled guy, six feet tall and probably weighing close to two thirty. He was not used to being unable to move around whomever he wanted. My augmentations made me strong enough to easily lift him over my head if I so desired, but I rarely had need to display the full measure of my strength. Even though we had been training together for weeks, none of them knew how strong I really was because gladiatorial combat isn't about brute strength; it's about weapon finesse and control. More importantly, it's about having good predictive judgment or instincts, which only comes with experience.

A few onlookers gathered as we were practicing in the middle of the yard, as opposed to our usual place to the side. I thought it was time for a little show. I've spent most of my time in Las Vegas being the turtle on the bottom of the pile, surrounded by fighters of extreme skill. Frankly, I felt the need to push back a little; I was an extremely dangerous person in the right environment, and I was tired of being the newbie.

"Let's make this interesting. Karas, Zuma, Diana—all of you grab one of the dull knives and let's see what happens. I'll put a lady on myself, and match any you put on yourselves if I lose!"

"Deal!" Karas roared, pulling out a knife and joining Zew on the sand. Diana and Zuma followed suit with similar cries.

"I'll need a little more space on this one...say we start forty feet apart?" I suggested. They acquiesced and moved deeper into the training yard. Karas cleared the practice area of another group of gladiators simply by walking into it and claiming it—he knew everyone would get out of his way when he wanted where they were standing. No one was foolish enough to dispute him when there was a weapon in his hand, even if it was blunted.

We bowed, and then they came at me.

I dove toward Karas first, driving a straight stab into his chest and blocking his knife arm with my shin while I twisted out of the way with a secondary jump toward Zuma. A collective gasp went through the crowd—Karas, the eight-time champion, had been killed in less than half a second! I smashed into Zuma with a whirl of arm blocks and a single slice across the back of his neck, before flipping back away from a rushing Zew. Another gasp ripped the crowd, and a straight-arm block and double side stab took down Zew the same way I'd "killed" him the first time. Diana proved the most troublesome, actually putting up three seconds of maneuvering before taking a killing blow. I'd taken all four of them down in less than ten seconds.

The crowd erupted in a cheer, and I got them chanting

"Tuna, tuna, tuna!" with a little persuasion and arm pumping. Both Karas and Zuma were laughing so hard tears gathered in the sides of their eyes. They willingly passed over their coins when I came to collect. Diana and Zew did the same, newfound respect in their eyes.

After that display, Zew didn't really feel like fighting anymore, so we just sat around and drank, listening to Karas and Zuma swap stories before saying our final goodbyes, passing through the turnstile one last time and surrendering our punch cards.

The last two days in Las Vegas were pensive. You know that feeling you get when you know you're leaving somewhere forever...you haven't left yet, but it feels like you've already gone? That feeling. I took the time to buy two desirables: three pounds of green coffee that I could roast and grind later and three pounds of mixed hard candy for the kiddos back at Deeplac. They might not keep for the rest of the trip, but I was going to try. I like seeing smiling faces on the little ones.

On my last night in town, I stopped by Crikloto's to see if he'd acquired any klarklon or power cells for me. The grin on his reptilian face spoke volumes, and we quietly ambled to his back room. "It took a while, but I found some," Crikloto said, lisping. "Not very much, but enough, yes?"

On a table were three different canisters. None of them fit my M1B, but if Marilyn or Elissa could figure out some way of moving the gas about, it would be as good as gold to me. I didn't recognize the two unlabeled containers, but the third was not only labeled but still factory-sealed. The power cells were also the wrong size, but their potential in the hands of Deeplac's tinkers was the same as the klarklon. Testing power cells for validity was much easier as they came with self-diagnostics.

I checked the power cells; two of them were below twenty-five percent, one was at ten percent. "These are nearly empty," I complained.

"They're very hard to find. Finding full ones is impossible," he countered in the age-old bargaining dance.

"Two of the klarklon containers are unidentifiable. There's no way to test them."

"Both are full! Tinker's honor!" He crossed his heart with all of his arms.

I scowled, not only because I didn't know if I could trust him—I probably couldn't—but because I had no idea how much all of this would cost. As a general rule, letting the seller set the price is a negotiating error. "What do you want for the three cells and the labeled klarklon container?" I submitted.

He looked surprised, but quickly recovered. "I have to have at least twenty eagles just to cover my costs."

"Done," I quickly assented, "but I'll need change." I pulled out a sixty-eagle House of Flores note and watched his reaction. Either I was a fool for paying so much or he was a fool for walking away from more coin by not naming a higher starting price—this is the balance of bargaining, where the elusive sweet spot is when we both walk away satisfied that we couldn't have gotten any more or paid any less. He hid his disappointment well, but his Gila monster hands felt sticky like a Gecko's when he doled out my change. I called the deal a draw—I probably overpaid, but considering I was walking away with the goods and forty more eagles that would spend anywhere, I could live with that. I packed everything away and went back for my final night at Hotel White House.

Chapter Eighteen

We Are the Road Crew

We woke well before dawn, as our last day in Las Vegas was bound to be busy. None of the other guests were up at that hour, so Diana, Zew, and I enjoyed a somewhat-leisurely breakfast before saying our goodbyes to Soledad and her family. All our possession in hand, we headed to the south gate to retrieve our weapons, which took some time; there was always a rush out of the city regardless of the time of day. It was an hour before we were outside of Vegas's gates.

Traveling along the walls, we made our way to the north gate and our House Flores passes gained us entrance into the north ward. It also garnered us an escort, one of the duke's guards, named Kendra. Apparently, she would be with us until we were on the caravan and out of the city. Judging by her dour demeanor, she must have drawn the short stick on duty assignment.

The north ward was largely open, and the few buildings—placed in a giant horseshoe around a huge clearing—were large bunkhouses, workshops, or warehouses. In the center rested a fully functioning gas station. I had a slight moment of "castaway sickness" when I spotted the lizard-descended sentient dressed in blue work coveralls casually pumping gas into an armored dune buggy covered with spikes. Around the edges of the clearing were piles of damaged vehicles being used for parts.

"You're earlier than you needed to be, so we'll wait here for about an hour. Once everything's ready, we'll join with the crew and you'll get the full walkthrough," Kendra explained as she led us into a rather cramped room in the smallest of the buildings and indicated that we should wait there. "Although you're paying customers, you're still expected to defend yourselves and that means you're also expected to defend the caravan." She paused to let that sink in. "You are the caravan, the caravan is you, and no one rides for free."

The brusque treatment surprised me—for a hundred eagles, I'd expected to be treated as VIPs. It was a tedious hour as none of us wanted to talk in front of Kendra and she refused to move from the door. Although outwardly indifferent to her responsibilities, I'm sure she was as glad as we were when she finally escorted us to a much larger space.

Orientation occurred in one corner of a high-ceilinged warehouse stuffed with wooden crates of various sizes and origins. Two hundred chairs faced an old-fashioned movable blackboard displaying a hand-drawn map of the caravan route with the Lawman's area clearly mapped out and identified by mile marker. Next to the blackboard were three vehicles stripped down to their seats and frames: two automobiles and one tractor-trailer cab. A plastic-and-metal table was on the other side of the blackboard.

We were the first to arrive, and Kendra led us to seats in the front row. "We put all the new travelers up front. You'd be wise to pay close attention once things get started." She left us, taking up guard on the warehouse entrance and monitoring us as cargo flowed in and out.

More sentients arrived over the next half hour until a quarter of the seats were filled. They came in dribs and drabs, some greeting familiar faces while others took their seats quietly. By the end of the hour, all the seats were filled and the instructor arrived, a rail-thin sentient with bat-like wings. He was carrying a clipboard in one hand and a pen in the other.

"All right, settle down," he began. "My name's Lorne. For most of you this lesson isn't really needed, but I see two dozen or so new faces among the crowd, so keep your yaps shut and let me get them the information you already know.

"Before we get started, can any of you newbies drive?"

I put my hand up as did two other sentients.

"You two are our new drivers," Lorne pointed to the other two. I wasn't sure if there were only two spots or if my purchased passage excused me of driver duty.

"Of those who don't know how to drive, how many of you have an idea of how a motorized vehicle works?" Six hands went up, including Diana's and Zew's.

"Good, that'll make the end of the orientation go quickly,"

he said, eying the clipboard. "Now that that's settled, let's gets started. First up—history. Fifty-nine years ago, the first motorized caravan set off from West Denver, delivering 9,000 gallons of gasoline for the tanks the duke had prepared. Ever since that day, motorized trade's gone back and forth between us and the various Colorado Kingdoms."

He paused and gathered his breath before continuing, "West Denver isn't a state anymore, but trade goes on after kingdoms fall. Your purpose, your goal, is to make sure the trade continues. The caravan lives forever!" Lorne's wings fluttered with the intensity of his speech, even though he must have given it a hundred times before.

"The task ahead of us isn't easy. After only a few years of trade, the first of the Red Line Raiders appeared and we learned of the Lawman's claim to the lands we traveled through. Over time, the power of the Raiders has waxed and waned, and now it appears they are gaining strength again. The most recent trip was the hardest fought in years and we expect the same for this one."

Lorne picked up a pointer from the lip of the blackboard. "The trip starts here," he said, pointing to Las Vegas, "and ends here, where the caravan splits into three groups." A spot west of Denver received the end of the pointer this time. "The trip takes about eighteen hours and ranges in speed from thirty mph to sixty mph. There are no stops on the trip, so when you've got to go, climb to the backend of your vehicle and make your business."

"And try not to let loose on anyone that's right behind you!" a voice yelled from the back. Laughter followed and another voice said, "I told you to stop riding our tail, didn't I?" to even greater laughter.

Lorne didn't say anything and let his stink eye calm down the jokers in the back. "There are a series of markers starting one mile outside of the Lawman's territory informing you to separate your ammunition from your firearm. If you choose not to, you'll be dead within a few minutes and your traveling companions will split your gear evenly, as we do with any who die along the road. Traveling companions share risks, they also share in the rewards. If you kill any of the Raiders and keep their bodies, you'll split their possessions among your companions. If combat takes you from one vehicle to another, you are now a companion to the sentients on that vehicle."

Lorne's voice sounded the cadence of military instructors throughout the world, making simple declarative sentences that stuck in the heads of even the densest listener. "All of the vehicles have expanded gas tanks and enough fuel to get you to your destination, but if your vehicle is damaged and requires additional gas, you will have to perform an on-road refueling. The Tanker One protectors know how to do this, provided you can keep a safe distance from the rear fueling nozzle attached to Tanker One. Tanker Two does not carry fuel in this direction; it carries olive oil, so it cannot refuel you. All vehicles contain towing chains in case another needs towing."

Olive oil, huh? The climate was a bit harsh for olive trees, so it must be coming in from California. I suppose they could also have groves around Lake Mead, if they're using one of the hardy genetically engineered varieties from my time. They'd have to be near the lake due to the increased water demands of that hybrid. Maybe that's what "water guard" meant on the wheel of misfortune outside the gate...it wasn't about guarding the water runs, it was about guarding the olive groves adjacent to the water. If they're shipping out thousands of gallons of olive oil every trip, that'd be a hell of a lot of trees—even the hybrid only puts out two or three gallons a year per tree.

Lorne continued speaking through my thoughts, "Your primary objective is to get the vehicle you are on to its destination. Your secondary objective is to help other vehicles get to their destination. If you fall off a vehicle, you will be left behind. You do not want to be left behind. If another vehicle's driver is killed or injured and you can drive, you are obligated to change vehicles and become the new driver. Those are the rules. Do not break them."

As he finished, another sentient walked up, carrying a heavy box he deposited on the plastic table. Lorne opened the box. "In exchange for your service, you will receive three eagles, one now, and two when you return. As I call your name, come forward and claim your pay."

He barked out each name from a list on his clipboard, and

one by one, each sentient claimed their coin. I only recognized a few of them, but Zew and Diana gave me a quiet rundown on those they recognized from the arena matches I'd missed. Once he finished and everyone put their pay away, he flipped the blackboard and tapped it with his pointer until everyone settled down. The backside of the board featured a visual list of all the vehicles with their crew list next to them.

"Here are your assignments. Find your crew and go through this door to the adjacent hanger." He strode to a nearby door and opened it. "Those of you who are new, please keep your seats and stay behind."

It took a while for the crowd to clear out, leaving only the new members behind. Lorne walked over to the three frame-only vehicles and waved us to circle up around them. "I'm going to demonstrate how each of these vehicles work," he said, climbing into the automatic vehicle first. "All the vehicles in the other hanger work like these do, regardless of how they look on the outside." He worked through the basics of driving a vehicle—automatic, standard, and tractor-trailer—using clear language and naming everything he touched as he went. It wasn't nearly thorough enough of an introduction, but it was a good step on the road for some of the new crewmembers who'd never been close to a working vehicle. Just being able to touch parts and name functional aspects removed some of the mystery.

Once everyone had a chance to mess around with the frame-only vehicles, Lorne moved us into the main hanger with the rest of the road crew. He stopped at the threshold. "You've got an hour to look around and familiarize yourself with the vehicle you've been assigned to. You should also become familiar with the other vehicles and caravaners, so proper communication can be maintained."

Once inside, the first vehicles in sight were two tractor-trailers pulling tankers, and they received the bulk of attention from the scurrying mechanics, indicating they were the heart of the caravan. Each cab and tank had large matching numbers painted upon them for easy identification. Both were fronted with cowcatchers, fabricated from scrap, that could clear any debris forward and out. The cabs were heavily armored with thick scrap, rendering them nigh impervious to typical hand-to-hand weapons. Thin spikes protruded periodically along the cabs to deter boarders. There were foot rails and handrails installed along the sides, allowing side guards to move from the cabs to the rear of the tanks while two small armored boxes—one near the cabs and the other on the rear—provided the side guard a modicum of safety, albeit only up to the waist. Stretching the full length of the top of the tankers, a crenellated metal walkway provided protection for a cluster of warriors. Unusually, the first tanker was a split tank allowing it to carry two liquids; the smaller of its two tanks being one-third the size of the larger.

Behind the tanker trucks stood two tractor-trailers with

box trailers. The box trailers were reinforced to accommodate the weight of the fighters atop them, but otherwise modified in the same fashion as the tankers.

Each tanker and box trailer had a crew of eleven: driver, backup driver, four side warriors, and five toppers. The tanker and trailer crews were the most experienced fighters on the caravan, and among the warriors, at least two on each crew were capable of driving the rig in case both drivers were knocked out of the picture.

On the far side of the box tractor-trailers rested a series of mixed-sized box trucks: four twenty-four-footers, five sixteen-footers, and three ten-footers. Each had an armored cab and small cowcatcher, like their larger brethren, along with the reinforced box and crenellations. All but the ten-footers had two side warriors. The twenty-four-footers had a crew of eight, the sixteen-footers a crew of six, and the ten-footers only had a crew of four—two drivers and two rooftop warriors.

Next up were two transport vehicles, one of which was our assignment. They were converted EMT rigs and heavily armored. Mounted atop our ride was a swivel turret with dual M240B medium machine guns entered from the box below. The other had a single SG-43 Goryunov—where the hell they'd found a WWII Russian weapon in the middle of the North American southwest was beyond me. They were rigged for side warriors with one of the armored "castles" on each back corner. They were crewed by five, so Diana and Zew took side warrior positions while I manned the turret. The transports were the only members of the caravan with built-in firearms: all the others were defended by the firearms of their passengers.

Loren noticed me checking out the M240Bs and answered my unspoken question, "You can fire the weaponry, but it costs an eagle for every twenty rounds. You're carrying 400 per barrel—you empty them, you owe us forty eagles. And it goes without saying, you can't have it loaded in the Lawman's territory." He had the look of someone that spent a fair amount of time having to say things that went without saying.

Past the two transports were eight chaser autos of various shapes. They were all small three-to-four passenger vehicles, all modified in distinctive ways that earned them their names: Hedgehog, Buzzkill, Tracker, Spike-O-Rama, Thunderhead, Conman, Son of Hedgehog, and Undertaker. The chasers were driven by the most-experienced drivers, but staffed by two of the least experienced warriors. They were expected to actively engage the Red Line Raiders whenever possible. I got the gut feeling they were considered expendable—they carried no cargo.

Last in the lot was the scout, named Slider, crewed by four of the duke's soldiers. It was the only anti-gravity vehicle of the bunch, and the crew claimed it could go several hundred miles an hour. Slider operated under a strict non-engagement policy; it went with the caravans to scout ahead and around them, and report back if the entire caravan was lost.

After securing our belongings in our vehicle—transport vehicles came with small footlockers for up to five people—I walked throughout the caravan and inspected the other trunks and cars. The interiors were unique, in part due to the variety of scrap available to the mechanics. The only thing they all shared was a fire extinguisher and a CB radio. It was good to know the convoy could share information up and down the line; the importance of communication on the road couldn't be overstressed. I wouldn't be surprised if that was responsible for reducing the Red Line Raiders' success rate—the speedy Slider was able to maneuver regardless of the terrain, and could communicate enemy tactics and coordinate a defense with the rest of the caravan. It would be hard for the Raiders to obfuscate their intentions for tactical gain.

I noticed a few ubiquitous changes that hinted at the continual back and forth with the Red Line Raiders. Like all pieces of military hardware, the vehicle's design reflected the combat history of the engagements that created them. For instance, every wheel well contained a heavy-duty cutting blade designed to slice through any wheel stoppers or axle catchers, and vehicles with electronics had their electrical cores hardened against minor EMP attacks, like what you'd get from the business end of an EMP cannon. Oh, and every tire was airless, of course—probably one of the first adjustments they'd made.

As I inspected each set of wheels, I introduced myself to

their crews. None of the warriors were terribly interested in me, but at least I put names to their faces, and with my abilities, all it takes is one introduction.

I spent the last ten minutes in our vehicle getting to know the driver, a near-human named Lorenzo, and the backup driver, his twin named Umberto. Thankfully they wore distinctive clothing so keeping them separate wasn't an issue. They had an easygoing feeling about them, but not enough to make me worry about their competence. They seemed surprised that I'd taken the time to get to know them; I got the feeling that most of the sentients who paid for transport didn't talk to "the help."

As the last minutes wound down, Lorne watched the clock. When it ticked over, he blew a whistle and ordered, "Time to get in the saddle and ride!"

Chapter Nineteen

The Roar of the Engines

The experienced caravaners let loose with a distinctive warbling howl, and the hanger filled with the roar of twenty-six combustion engines. Smoke and exhaust plumed throughout the hanger, gears engaged, and we exited as a single giant block. Once out of the hanger, we lined up in the positions we'd keep for the entire trip in the huge clearing that took up most of the north ward.

Slider started out in front and would continually circle the caravan. Two chasers, Thunderhead and Tracker, lead the way, followed by the tanker trucks and the box trailers. To the left and right of the four big rigs were Hedgehog and Son of Hedgehog, their spikes easily capable of spearing any Raiders hanging on to another vehicle. Our transport was after the big rigs and behind us was a dual line of box trucks, six long. To the left of the box trucks were the chasers Buzzkill and Conman, while to the right was Spike-O-Rama and the Undertaker. Last in line was the other transport, running empty of inhabitants but stuffed to the gills with trade goods. They did have a gunner, however, and it was one of the duke's guards, so I assumed they had free reign on ammo to fire their turret gun.

Once we'd lined up, the north gates rolled open. I slid open the armored window to let some air in as we tested the CBs to make sure they were all working. The test was the last of the checks, and then we were off, leaving behind a cloud of brown-red dust as the only indication we were ever there in the first place. The first ten minutes were pure excitement—I hadn't traveled much faster than twenty mph in the past two years, and I'd forgotten the utter exhilaration of speed.

However, my buzz was nothing compared to that of Zew and Diana; I suspected they'd never gone faster than horseback their entire lives. Unadulterated joy suffused them both as they bounced between standing up in the turret—heads popping like meerkats out of a moving metal den—and pushing their arms and heads out of the sliding steel windows on their side of the transport.

They calmed down after a while and I caught a whiff of envy in Diana's face as she realized this was part of my past. Up till now, she'd taken everything I'd said about my world with a grain of salt; stories from the ancients with little relevance to the present. But at forty-five mph, she viscerally experienced something from my prior life and maybe started to appreciate a little of what I'd lost by coming to the land beneath the shattered moon. I'd like to think she came to some sort of understanding during the early part of our ride, but I don't know her well enough to be sure and I respected her too much to ask.

Once they'd settled in, I took the opportunity to teach them about fully automatic weapons using the M240Bs as examples. We didn't fire them, of course, but if they needed to fire them on this trip, they'd know how. It didn't take very long, and we spent the next hour watching the barren desert roll by while listening to the wind, the rumble of the engines that surrounded us, and the constant banter on the CBs. The patter of the drivers showed that they were a separate group within the group.

The relaxed tone broke with an announcement from the scout: "This is Slider. We've got dust trails to the west, about three miles up."

The message cut through the chatter. "Time for you to go out on guard," Umberto said through the small sliding window that separated the cab and the back of the transport vehicle. We nodded and I took the turret while Diana and Zew took to the protected areas on the back corners outside the vehicle. From up top, I could see the barest streak of dust from the northwest. I dropped into the back, pulled out my binoculars, and had a go at it with the highest magnification.

The dust trail was from a single vehicle: a modified Ariel Atom. Traveling around ten to twenty mph, it moved on large, knobby, off-road tires and was raised nearly a foot up. The passenger was staring back at me through her own set of binoculars. I threw her the finger and got one in return. I ducked into the back and told Umberto what I'd seen. He relayed the information to the other drivers, "We've made Roadrat as the sign maker, Slider." He turned toward me and explained, "Roadrat's the main scout for the Raiders. She's a nasty piece of work—can move fire about with her mind. She's the reason why we don't use fire to defend ourselves anymore: she just puts it right out or sends a bit of it back our way."

"Why don't they use fire on us?"

He grinned. "Sometimes they do, but our fire extinguishers usually work! Anyway, they want loot, not kindling."

I nodded and returned to the turret. Roadrat must have seen what she wanted because she was now barreling to the north. According to Lorne's map, we had a half hour until we entered the Lawman's territory. A short three miles after that was the Glendale Grind, the first of many squeezes where the terrain pinched in around the road and provided cover for hidden raider vehicles. There were dozens of squeezes along the route, and according to Lorenzo, we should expect trouble to pour out of at least three or four of them.

I conveyed Roadrat's retreat to Umberto, and the thought of the Lawman prompted me to double-check the chambers of the M240Bs to make sure there weren't any rounds in them. They were clear, their ammunition belts resting on the inside of the transport in their respective ammo cans. I told Zew and Diana our situation and they remained hunkered down. I think they enjoyed being on the outside of the transport more than the inside.

Eventually I lost eyes on Roadrat and put my binoculars back in the storage area to keep them from being damaged; it would only take me a moment to retrieve them if I needed them again. Twenty minutes later, I saw the first of the Lawman's markers and double-checked Zew and Diana's rifles for them. It was a bit presumptive, but they were outside and wouldn't know. I felt better knowing they were in the clear.

I'd put my rifle and ammunition in separate storage units so they were good, but I didn't want to let the M1B out of my sight. I removed the power cell and put it in my left front pocket along with the klarklon cell; even though the M1B wouldn't work without power, I didn't want the Lawman to catch me on a technicality. I buttoned the pocket for safekeeping; I'd had buttons and buttonholes stitched into my front pockets when I arrived in Las Vegas to avoid theft. Diana called me paranoid, but I hadn't been pickpocketed, had I?

We entered the Lawman's domain shortly thereafter, passing by a series of markers that counted down the distance. Nothing felt different, nothing looked different, but if everyone was to be believed, a loaded gun was now a death sentence.

"Glendale Grind coming up!" Umberto yelled. Ahead of us, Thunderhead and Tracker had just turned a hard right, slowing down in the process. As the tankers took the turn, the Red Line Raiders attacked, launching themselves from behind an assortment of hillocks and depressions. Eight automobiles the size of our chasers, containing a driver and two warriors each, joined our caravan.

They opened with a peppering of arrows to no effect, which was to be expected given the noticeable lack of missile weapons on the experienced caravaners. It's hard to shoot a bow with any accuracy in these conditions; the bumps on the road were unpredictable for those of us riding upon it, and the terrain was worse for those riding next to it.

Our chasers closed to protect our flanks and Hedgehog and Son of Hedgehog proved their value immediately, spearing a driver and a warrior on one of their many spikes. The driverless vehicle spun off several hundred yards before the secondary driver could get control of it, barely avoiding a crash in the process.

Two of the raider vehicles maneuvered between the chasers and closed on a box truck, but the warriors on the truck kept them at bay with their spears. After a few seconds of sparring, the Raiders pulled out of their compromised position between the box truck and chasers and peeled off of the caravan. The other vehicles followed suit and soon a separate caravan of Raiders drove a quarter mile behind us, sealing off the road in that direction and pacing us like a pack of wolves. The caravaners let out another of their distinctive warbling howls at the raider's retreat, but I suspected the Raiders pacing us would roar forward during the next squeeze to join more of their kind attacking from the flanks.

The next section of the highway was in better condition

and we sped up to fifty mph. We were outside easy scavenging distance and carcasses of old vehicles started appearing, most of them damaged from fire as well as exposure. There's something about ruins that calls to firebugs. You expect a certain amount of it from the practical side—we all need to keep warm—but much of it was clearly for kicks. I get it, I really do—destruction on a mass scale has its appeal. Something in my gut leapt with joy when the Lancaster Building came crashing down, but I certainly didn't blow it up just because it was there. I don't think I could say the same about firebugs.

After fifteen minutes at our faster speed, Umberto yelled, "Riverside Squeeze coming up!" and the convoy slowed down once more. We had been driving on a flat plateau since Glendale, and according to my internal map, the Riverside Squeeze was a four-mile-long 800-foot descent down the side of the Virgin River, pocked with hiding places for vehicles. The Raiders following us narrowed the gap down to two hundred yards and everyone in the caravan readied themselves for the coming attack.

We broke off the plateau and headed east down the long slope when the unmistakable sound of heavy machine-gun fire ripped through the air. I ducked down and desperately looked for the weapon, finding it atop one of the rocky points to our north. The barrel blazed, strafing the length of the caravan with hundreds of rounds. The **brrrap** of the gun was quickly followed by yells of pain, squealing tires, and the sound of crashing vehicles ahead and behind us.

I barely had time to duck into the transport when it started leaning to the left and tipped over, sliding along the pavement. I hit hard against the front of the transport interior, hoping Zew had jumped free before the road caught on the metal box he manned. We slowed in the skid but went spinning as another vehicle crashed into us from behind. The barrage of bullets swept by again, creating more shafts of light in the darkened hull.

I shook my head, clearing it from the wreck, and immediately popped out of the turret to check on Diana. She was uninjured, having hooked her feet into the stabilizers in the side warrior castle just before we wrecked. She jumped off the transport in a panic, headed straight for Zew, who was lying limp two hundred feet behind us, just off the side of the road. Vehicles were rushing by him, slowly getting closer and closer as they tried to navigate around our downed trunk and the wreck of one of the tanker trunks in front of us.

Why are they shooting at the tanker trunks? How were they shooting to begin with? Where was the Lawman!

Chapter Twenty

Survival

An angry and wounded howl erupted from the cab of the transit. "They killed Lorenzo!" Umberto yelled as he fled the cab through the window. "The bastards killed Lorenzo!" I would have responded, but I was diving into the transit box to grab the Panjang Pharmaceuticals medikit. As I dug through the wreckage in the box, Umberto joined me briefly, grabbing an ammo can before darting out. I finally found the kit and heard the distinctive click of one of the M240Bs being released from its locks.

Brrrap! The heavy gun fired again, adding more rays of light in the back of the cabin and missing me by mere inches before it moved down the ranks toward the other vehicles. I dove for the turret and crawled out. Umberto had already loaded the M240B before I could warn him.

"I'm going to kill that bastard!" he yelled at me, seeing the look on my face. "And the Lawman can go to hell! Where is he now? The coward!" He opened fire on the rocky point to our north and the gun attacking us silenced. I don't know if that was because Umberto hit the shooter, or if he was just reloading. Up the road, I saw Tanker One was down. From its dual tanks olive oil and gasoline spilled out onto the road, flowing over the littered remains of the crew. Box Trailer One was down as well. Both looked like they'd been hit hard, as none of the bodies were moving.

I looked down the road. Diana had reached Zew and dragged him away from the following box trucks, but the final transport had just passed her and would be passing me in seconds, leaving us to face the eight Red Line Raiders' automobiles that followed.

"Shoot the damn Raiders, Umberto! They're upon us! Shoot the Raiders!" I yelled, pointing down the road with my spear at the approaching enemies. If he'd signed his death warrant, at least he could go down trying to save some lives. I sprinted toward Zew with all the speed I could muster and hoped Umberto would listen, otherwise there wouldn't be a lot of hope for any of us.

Umberto turned the gun down the road, but in his anger and grief, he failed to control his weapon and hit my left shoulder, sending me sprawling onto the ground from the impact. The medikit flew out of my hand, as did my spear. The hard landing dislodged my M1B from its holster as I twisted to a stop, face down on the pavement. The crashing I heard ahead let me know he'd taken out at least one of the Red Line Raiders' vehicles.

I rose as quickly as I could, testing my screaming shoulder in the process. It held and took my full weight, informing me that nothing vital was hit—probably just a graze. I grabbed my spear and medikit, reluctantly leaving the M1B behind since I didn't have time to fix my torn holster. As I hustled, I noticed my buttoned pocket had also torn open in my tumble and the power cell and klarklon canister had fallen to the ground as well. If I lived through this, I could pick them up later; I had to get to Zew as seconds could make a difference.

I'd covered a few more steps toward him and Diana when the sky rumbled unnaturally, darkening like a thunderstorm in a handful of seconds. I felt a cold breeze pass through. The oncoming Raiders panicked, slamming on their breaks and turning around as quickly as they could.

Over the noise of squealing tires and whining engines, over the blaring of the M240B, over Diana's yelling, I heard the galloping of a horse matching the beat of the clicks from Umberto's gun as its ammunition ran out. Out of nowhere, a horse and its rider appeared. All of us froze in place, unable to move, paralyzed by the fear emanating from the spirit we faced.

The horse was emaciated, its white hide drawn tight around its bones. Its hooves didn't touch the ground, and where it stepped, a glowing azure haze remained, floating in the air just above the surface. Its eyes were the same flaming blue, and they matched the pinprick flames that served as eyes for the Lawman.

The Lawman was as skeletal as his horse, his dark skin the color of old leather. His clothes were straight out of the

Old West, and a dusty flat-brimmed Stetson crowned his head. Upon his breast, a shining silver star caught the light, regardless where the sun stood in the sky. He slowed his horse as he approached Umberto, whose fearful fingers dropped his weapon to the ground.

"You do not have the right to bear arms," the Lawman said. He drew his ancient .45 from its holster faster than the eye could see, and then Umberto fell to the ground, shot dead between the eyes.

And then all of us could move again.

I sprinted away from the Lawman and toward Zew, medikit and spear hindering my speed, but I only made it a few steps before I was interrupted once more, this time by a flashing light and burning sensation around my wrist. Efte's bracelet was consumed, delivering its promised warning—the shadow people who follow me, the souls of everyone I'd killed, were trying to return the favor.

I turned and found the cold cerulean flames in the eye sockets of the Lawman fixed upon me. I dropped my medikit and spear and raised my hands, showing I was unarmed. His gaunt horse took a step toward me, and that's when I noticed the power cell I'd dropped slowly moving toward the handle of the M1B, dragging a small trail of dirt as it went. It was mere feet away when the cover to the power chamber popped open on the blaster. That's when I understood—they were going to load my weapon and frame me!

I was too far to reach the blaster in time, so I grabbed my spear and threw it, silently praying that my instructors had trained me well. Before it even landed, I was sprinting back toward the gun; the weapon flew true, landing in the dirt by the handle of the M1B, blocking access to the power chamber. Under the baleful eye of the Lawman, I dove just in time to grab the now-moving blaster as it edged past the spear blade in an effort to join with the power cell. As my hand wrapped around it, I quickly closed the power chamber and covered it with my palm just to be certain. I also retrieved the power cell and klarklon canister, pushing them deep into my button-less pockets.

My shoulder sharply protested, but I ignored it and pushed off the ground once more. Running toward my injured friend, I grabbed the dropped medikit as I went. As I arrived next to the distraught Diana, the sky cleared and I glanced back to discover the Lawman absent. If the raiders had fled before him, they'd surely be coming back now that he was gone. I had very little time.

Zew was unconscious, face up on his back. His nose and left ear were gone, scraped off as he slid across the road, but his eyes appeared uninjured. The road rash extended down his body from shoulder to hip, and his left humerus had a compound fracture. His breathing was fine, but as he'd pissed himself, I worried about other spinal nerve damage.

"You've got to fix him, Stonewall!" Diana yelled at me,

holding on to her spear as she rose from the ground. She faced the Raiders, who'd just started turning around. "I'll hold them off. I'll hold all of them off." Her voice was a bulwark before which even the ocean would yield.

"I don't have time to do it here, but I can do it," I told her, quickly clunking open the medikit to retrieve the Huang Immobilizer. I freed it from the package and poured it over Zew. The liquid expanded, flowing over his whole body before transforming into an aerogel which then pneumatized, effectively immobilizing and cushioning his whole body in less than ten seconds. While it hardened, I pulled out an adrenaline shot and jammed it into my neck and stuffed my M1B into the medikit and forced it closed—I had to have my hands free and my holster was trashed.

Once the cocoon set, I put the medikit on Zew and lifted him, carrying his stiffened body in a cradle hold. "Let's go!" Diana looked back and if she was surprised by what I'd done to Zew, she didn't show it. We reached the transport, and I placed Zew upon the ground—the Raiders were less than a quarter mile away.

"Help me flip this!" I yelled at Diana, putting my hands under the overturned transport. I lifted with all my might and the full power of the adrenaline I administered hit my body. Normally I could deadlift a thousand pounds, but I needed to exceed that by ten and I—Arrrrrggggh!—tipped over the transport with a massive drug-fueled yell, startling Diana in the process, who was applying all her strength as well to right the transport.

I moved to the driver's side as I barked clipped instructions to Diana, "In through the turret, open the back door, put Zew in, close door!" I pulled Lorenzo out of the driver's seat and checked for keys. Thankfully, they were still in the ignition. I jumped in and tried the engine, which turned on the first try.

Oh hell, we just might make it out of here.

I looked back through the sliding cab door into the box and saw Diana push Zew into the back. "Hold on!" I shouted over the blare of the voices on the CB, and took off as fast as I could. The Red Line Raiders were less than a hundred yards away. She held on, one hand gripping a ceiling strap while the other kept Zew from sliding out due to the acceleration. After a few seconds, she jumped to the back and sealed the doors with a solid thunk of the metal bar that kept them closed.

"They're on us! Turret!" I called out as I swung to the left and right, inhibiting an easy board for the raiders. In the rear view window, I saw Diana grab an extra spear and pass into the turret. I kept twisting to the left and right as two of the Red Line Raider chasers paced me, jumpers ready to board the transport where our side warriors should have been. The left side was mangled and proving difficult, but the right side was intact and after two sways, a raider had jumped on us, clinging to the handholds while spearing at Diana.

I don't know if she killed him or if he killed himself, but he was flopping down the road less than a second later. Given her fury, I suspect Diana directly offed him. Hands shaking from the adrenaline, I took a second to calculate how far behind we were from the rest of the convoy. Everything had happened in less than three minutes, and we were less than four miles behind the rest of the caravan. I punched the pedal and counted on my superior driving skills to keep us safe through the road debris.

It was a solid decision, as the Raider on our right called off his pursuit due to my increased speed. The chaser on our left was more daring, pulling slightly ahead of my cab and opening himself to a potential PIT maneuver. Before I could pull the wheel, a Raider jumped onto the cab. The warrior held on to my door and jabbed a knife at my face through the viewing slit in the door armor. I turned hard to the right to swing him out and off balance while I punched with my left hand, breaking his neck as I connected to his jaw. When I brought my hand back to the wheel, I saw it was broken as well; the fifth metacarpal slumped in a textbook boxer's fracture. I didn't feel a thing—I wasn't feeling my bullet wound either—but I knew I would once the adrenaline wore off.

"They're dropping back!" Diana yelled as the slid out of the turret. "They're going back for the other vehicles they downed." She set her spear down and turned toward Zew. "What did you do to him?"

"I couldn't do anything; I just had to immobilize him to reduce the chance of paralyzation."

"What do you mean? Did I hurt him when I moved him?" she questioned frantically.

"You had to move him, otherwise he would have been run over. There wasn't anything else you could have done. You did the right thing," I reassured her, trying extra hard to keep my voice calm while the adrenaline still jackhammered inside me. "Once we catch up and I can pull another driver in here, I'm going to look over him closely and see what I can do. That shouldn't be more than ten minutes, so just hold on, okay."

Now that we were in the clear, I grabbed the CB. Diana's face poked through the open slit, listening in. "This is Transport DeLuxe and we're searching for a driver. We've lost Lorenzo and Umberto and are willing to split their possessions with any willing to drive for us. I have injured aboard and am pressed for time. Come back."

There was radio silence for a brief moment before a clear message came through, "Transport DeLuxe, this is Tanker Two. Any word on the others?"

"I think they're all dead. We barely made it out. No one else was moving."

"10-4. I've got a sentient here who'll drive for you. Pull up to the side and let him board."

"Affirmative. I'll be there in five," I responded. "We'll be there soon," I repeated through the opening, "and then I'll do what I can. If you'd open the medikit and have it ready for me, that'll save a bit of time." I knew better than to tell Diana not to worry or have her sit and wait. She nodded and rearranged the jumbled contents of the box to closer to its original bearings.

It took a little over seven minutes to reach Tanker Two, and another two minutes to effect a driver switch, which involved me climbing out of the driver's side to the roof to enter the box via the turret. Under the apprehensive eye of Diana, I grabbed the Nguyen mobile diagnostic and scanned Zew from head to toe. Once I got the results, I quickly informed Diana.

"In addition to his facial and skin damage, he's got two linear skull fractures, a fractured C7—one of the bones in his spine—and a compound fracture of the left humerus as well as an Iliac wing fracture—a bone in his pelvis—and a fracture of his left femur. The transport must have landed on him when it tipped." Her face fell and the color beneath her green scales paled. "The good news is that he doesn't have any internal organ damage other than a concussion and there's no signs of internal bleeding, which is frankly miraculous, so I'm going to apply some medications and treatment that should work. However," I looked at her carefully, "he may not take to the medicines I'm going to use. They were designed for sentients like me, not like you or him or Broagh. They may not work as well or at all. There is also the possibility they may make everything worse."

"It can't be worse than this," she said without hesitation. "Do it."

I nodded and got to work. Diana quietly watched the entire time, except for when she had to defend the transport from another raider attack which occurred about an hour into proceedings.

Although the medikit was designed as an emergency battlefield tool, it was from the late 23rd century, so its scope and capabilities were impressive. The first thing I did was something I wouldn't normally do: put him under heavy sedation from which he wouldn't wake up for at least twenty hours. My practice wasn't to sedate concussions as a general rule, but the medikit recommended using one of their meds to do exactly that, so I trusted in the knowledge of a hundred plus years of medical research and advancement after my time and did what it told me to do. Additionally, I knew Zew didn't want to be awake for what came next.

The hardest part was resetting his compound fracture well enough to let the kit do its magic. Getting part of the cocoon to retract and then finagling his bones back into place while working against his damage resistance was difficult, even with my enhanced strength. Someone not as strong wouldn't have stood a chance—son of a bitch was tough hell. The forces that busted him up so badly would have just smeared another sentient into pulp.

By the time I finished, his missing ear and nose had regrown and his skin regenerated, his fractures were set and partially healed. The medikit brought the bones to about 50% healed or five weeks' worth of natural healing, give or take. He'd need five or six weeks of additional healing to get to full health, but I suspected Zew healed faster-than-normal in addition to being damage resistant, so it may only be two or three weeks. After two hours of work, the Nguyen Mobile Diagnostic said everything was on the up and up, so I informed Diana that he'd recover.

"So, no bad reactions?" she asked.

"None so far, so I don't think there's going to be any, but I'll keep watching him."

"Thanks, Stonewall. I owe you."

I didn't argue with her and instead just nodded and packed away the kit. I did, however, plan on using this in my defense if they ever found out about Cara. No Cara, no medikit, no Zew...so maybe my decision to save an AI wasn't so bad after all.

Three hours later, we fended off another attack, bringing our number of conflicts up to four, the number that the now-deceased Umberto said was the most common. It was a half-hearted affair at best and we shrugged it off, although one of our numbers was killed in the process. We didn't face another attack until exiting the Lawman's territory.

Exiting the territory presented the best opportunity for the Red Line Raiders, because they could take positions beyond the Lawman's territory and snipe at us while we were still in his domain. The caravan's solution was darkness; the runs were timed so that we traveled that last mile during the darkest time of night, around 3:00 a.m. Exiting was a straight shot down the highway at seventy mph and we fared better than the tractor-trailers in front of us who took the brunt of the fire. One of the secondary drivers was hit and killed, but other than that, the caravan came through, and once we were on the other side, our return fire set the Raiders packing.

The rest of the trip was uneventful and the sky brightened as we split into groups, each heading to a different Colorado Kingdom. Diana spent most of the time in the turret. I don't think she'd ever seen mountains before. I left her to it as my gut warned me she was well pissed that Zew had gotten himself hurt and it was his fault that they weren't sharing the sight together. I'm sure he wouldn't be the first person to wake up after a serious injury who had to apologize, even if it wasn't entirely justified.

Epilogue

"Where am I?" Zew asked groggily, and then followed up with, "What the hell is this thing?" He was referring to the immobilization cocoon. Only his left arm was free, from when I'd set it, and it was now in an old-fashioned plaster cast.

"You're in a hospital," I answered. Just saying it made me happy. The Library had an honest-to-god hospital, with honest-to-god staff—I'd quizzed them and they got most of my questions right. It might not be up to my time regarding medical knowledge, but it was real. The entire Library was, by far, the most advanced place I'd seen beneath the shattered moon.

"What's a hospital?"

"It's a place where you can rest while you heal. You just about died out there. I put that thing around you so you wouldn't move while you were unconscious. You'd broken your back and if you'd moved, you could have been paralyzed. It can come off soon…probably within a few days, depending on how your back heals."

"Is Diana alive?"

"Yes. She just stepped out for a bit. She's been here the whole time—said she needed some air."

"Good," he sighed with relief. "Don't want to lose her."

"And I don't want to lose you either, you asshole!" Diana spoke as she entered the room. "What happened out there, you catch a bad case of stupid? Don't have the sense to get out from under falling vehicles anymore? Making me all worried…and you missed the mountains in the morning sunlight!"

I took that as my cue to leave. Zew's voice stopped me at the door, "Thanks for coming back for me."

"Caravan's got their rules; I've got mine. Plus, Diana would have killed me," I joked and make a quick exit. No need to draw any of her ire my way. I strode down the hospital corridor and out into the sunlight.

"Hello, are you there? Stonewall?" Elissa said to me.

I quickly drew my knife and looked around before realizing the voice was in my head.

"Sorry," I apologized to a passing sentient I'd startled with my weapon. "Hearing voices in my head," I reassured him.

"Stonewall, can you hear me?" Elissa said again.

I sheathed the KM6800 and smiled. She'd fixed it. The Deeplacers had found my bug and Elissa had fixed it.

That's my girl!

THE END

Stonewall will next appear in *Stonewall Against the Center Sea.*